D1216526

"**M**uch more than a guidebook to the art of soulmaking, Michael Grosso's new volume sparkles with seminal insights and mind-stretching speculations concerning the soul-building potential of close encounters of the strange kind. Grosso's narrative gifts are superb and the stories he tells beguile us with their undeniable mysteries like an unforgettable exotic perfume."

Kenneth Ring, Ph.D.
Professor of Psychology,
University of Connecticut

Author of *Heading Toward Omega*

Also by Michael Grosso

The Final Choice
Frontiers of the Soul

SOULMAKER

True stories from the far side of the psyche

Michael Grosso

Foreword by Whitley Streiber

HAMPTON ROADS
PUBLISHING COMPANY, INC.

To my mother

For information, write:

Hampton Roads Publishing Co., Inc.
891 Norfolk Square
Norfolk, VA 23502

Or call: 804-459-2453
    FAX: 804-455-8907

If this book is unavailable from your local bookseller, it may be obtained directly from the publisher. Call toll-free 1-800-766-8009 (or-
ders only).

ISBN 1-878901-21-4

10 9 8 7 6 5 4 3 2 1

Printed in the United States of America

Contents

Foreword

by Whitley Strieber

It may be that everything we have ever thought about the soul is wrong. The mythology of religion, the sense that all present discovery is rediscovery, the pantheon of shadows that have in the past shaped our knowledge of the inner world—perhaps all of it is wrong.

But not entirely. When we have seen the soul clear, we may look back and say, yes, we can understand how those illusions arose.

There are stories beginning to be whispered among us, extraordinary stories of experiences that go beyond the physical, beyond the psychic, even beyond the mystical. Something is changing; the lights are turning on in this dark world. For the first time mankind is beginning to see the soul directly instead of perceiving only its reflections. We are, in short, learning to face ourselves and see ourselves as we are.

For five hundred years there have been two enormous negative forces at work in western culture. By attempting to deny our true nature, they have ended up by driving us finally into direct contact with it. We have not come here on an easy path; we are here because we are desperate.

The first of these negative forces is generally called rationalism, but might better be called denial. It masquerades as the belief that the immediately perceivable physical world is the only world, but its actual function is to support the idea that lives when the body dies, and thus the soul need not be responsible for how it conducts its life.

Reinforcing this idea has been a negative view of ourselves. We have, since monks in the middle ages began circulating demon-treatises, been taking an increasingly antagonistic attitude toward ourselves. It has reached a point where positive cultural icons must be pulled down at all costs. Thomas Jefferson kept slaves, Leonardo hallucinated, Mother Teresa is a harridan in the convent. The daily news is a ritual of self-deprecation, history is a compendium of disasters. In truth, Western civilization is a long journey toward economic plenty and common justice. But our histories *read like* a compendium of disasters.

The general trend of history has been upward, always, and now that we stand ready to spread our wings and soar, we have become obsessed with what is wrong with us.

Why do we hide from our own glory? Because it is a heavy responsibility to live up to one's own greatness. To accept ourselves as we are means that we must admit that we have value and importance, and that the way we live our lives matters. If we admit that the soul exists, we must change fundamentally; we must begin to lead examined lives.

This book is about one man's journey into the world of the soul. He has discovered the edges of an ancient freedom, the fact that we are each of us packed with unrealized potential, and the painful truth that it takes hard work to realize this potential. We have tried to blind our own in-seeing eyes, so we will not have to face the fact that living life can and must be the work of a craftsman or even an artist. We are not here by random choice, nor by the blind action of chemicals in the earth; we were not sent, we did not simply appear. We are here for aesthetic reasons: Each of us is crafting a soul.

It is not an accident that scientists, who are most closely associated with the great engines of destruction we have invented to serve our deep fear of worthlessness, would also be the most fiercely soul-blind. But this blindness cannot prevail. Physics has begun to send messages from the numinous world directly into the minds of the most determinedly sightless. The world is turning on its ear; rationalism is coming to seem irrational.

We cannot escape the presence of the soul, and we will not escape it. Deep within ourselves, below all the artificial self-hate, below the games of evil and the history-long dream of worthlessness, lies an invincible certainty that we have value, even that it is worth it to the tired old earth to bear our heavy presence.

Soulmaker suggests a possible future: When we begin to see into the world of the soul, we find that it is richly peopled with event, personality and being. Somebody looks out at us.

The curtain between the living and the world of the dead is falling. In a hundred years, death will not be viewed as an ending but as a passage. The needs and hungers of the fragile dead will be known, we will rescue the wanderers, we will take the hands of the leaders there; love will ordinarily cross the boundaries of the physical, and death will not separate lovers but deepen their embrace.

We will be able to design our lives rather than simply fall into them, and we will remember where we came from and where we are going. We will have learned to preserve the spontaneity of experience that is so essential to the growth of the soul while at the same time maintaining conscious awareness of our aim. In short, we will become craftsmen at the work of building and enriching our souls, and some of us will have begun to become artists. There will be a million Buddhas, the journey of the murdered God—Christ's journey—will be correctly understood and lived as it should be lived by everyone, and the voice will move in the land speaking as it did to Mohammed, to us all.

This is not an impractical vision, but a statement of fact. The corner has been turned, we will find our place, we will take wing.

There will come the discovery that the soul is not a given; we can die without making our souls, or with our souls unfinished, and sink back into the nascence of mankind, or await rebirth and another chance. But this can be a long wait. The species must first produce an infant whose genetic makeup exactly fits the potentials of the waiting soul, for that soul to return to life. And then it must try again to overcome the obstacles that defeated it the last time. The process is slow now, we spend many centuries on the wheel of life. But, if we were true craftsmen of the soul, *living* our lives intentionally instead of depending on random chance for growth, it would all go much faster. The ordeal of death and rebirth would reveal itself as a form of ecstacy.

We will soon discover empirical evidence not only that the soul exists, but that the world literally cannot go on without every one of us full and complete and intact, and that we must continue to ride the wheel of life until every spirit is free. Then the living will take on the mission of the dead, to free those who cannot free themselves. We will truly become our brothers' keepers.

We will conduct our lives as craftsmen and artists, not in the blundering, desperate and fear-filled manner of today. We will see beyond good and evil, and realize that the dark of life also is beautiful, that the skulls of Kali smile.

This is not a vision, it is a simple statement of future history. There is no reason to hide it, because this much of the tapestry has already been woven. What will we find when we become true soulmakers? What songs will we sing when we have faced our reality, the glory of mankind? It is easy to consider oneself a sinner—or, better, nothing but a mortal lump. How much more difficult to face one's greatness, and dare to begin the journey up Jacob's ladder. When we see ourselves from this new perspective, it will finally become possible to understand what our prophets meant when they said that we were all one, that there were no strangers among us.

It is easy to say that the discovery of the soul is nothing new. But what is happening now is quite new. The objective presence of the soul will no longer be deniable. We are no longer looking at its effects, but at the thing itself. No more myths, only the story of the soul-as-it-is.

We are finding out that we are a tremendous mystery. Are we a fragmented god just now awakening from a long dream of mortality, or are we the mind of a planet, or the toys of enigmatic creators, or anguished, conscious machines, or fallen angels? We do not know what we are. We do not know the nature of the extraordinary world of the soul, only that it is apparently there, that it is ancient and richly alive, and that it is calling us now, all of us, and we cannot resist the call.

We are already embarked on our journey, indeed, we have been for five thousand years. That is what history is about. History is when we take up our belongings and embark upon the Tarot's journey of the Fool. However, something has changed. The other beasts of the Tarot have joined us, the Hermit with his lantern to guide our way, the Magician with his tools to help us, the wise woman beckoning us at once toward the stars and into the shadowy deeps of self.

Shimmering on the horizon is the end of history as we know it. Books are being written that change minds, that enable us to drop the chains at last and go to the far side of the psyche: That is where the true stories are.

—Whitley Strieber

You would not find out the boundaries of soul, even by travelling along every path: so deep a measure does it have.

Heraclitus

Introduction
The Mystery of Soul

This book is about exploring the boundaries of soul—a process I call soulmaking. The boundaries of soul are unknown, says the Greek philosopher, Heraclitus. In the following pages, we examine this idea in some detail—by means of stories from the far side of the psyche.

The idea of soul has fallen on bad times. Under the spell of modern scientific materialism, we have come to think of soul—of mind and consciousness—as *nothing but* a by-product of the brain and nervous system. People, in effect, are reduced to mere physical objects, trapped in time and space, and caged inside the borders of sense experience.

2

Heraclitus had a broader view of our nature. At the core of our selves, the ancients pictured something called soul. Soul, a powerful though indefinite concept, meant many things to early people. Soul was the vital essence of a human being: the lord of the body and the seat of wisdom. It was the unseen source of life, the wellspring of inner strength, the revealer of meaning. And soul was the vehicle of the self—a body of light that travelled to other worlds of dreamtime and afterdeath.

Soul was our most precious possession. Above all, Socrates said, take care of your soul. Be at odds with the whole world, said the wise Greek, but never be at odds with your soul. And Jesus made the same point: "What does it profit a man if he gains the whole world and loses his soul?"

Indeed, people once believed we could lose our souls: A curse or spell might do the trick, the ill wish of some spirit we once wronged, an evil glance from an envious person. Soul life was precarious business.

Nowadays, we talk of our lives being depressed, our jobs boring us to death, our marriages wasting in unquiet desperation. The words may differ but people still have the "loss of soul" experience.

In early societies, it was the shaman's job to retrieve lost souls. In ours, where soul is put down as a figment of fancy, we have to be our own shamans. Being our own shamans is another way of talking about being soulmakers.

3

Modern science has scrapped the idea of soul. Why? It's a hard thing to study in the laboratory. Soul is systematically elusive, and resists exact definition. As Heraclitus said, you cannot find or measure its boundaries.

But for Science what isn't measurable isn't real. Our fluid inner realities are neither measurable nor dissectible; so science tends to judge them unreal. Since Galileo, the significance of soul has eroded. The world revealed by Newton was a world without soul. Descartes the philosopher took the soul out of nature; Watson the psychologist took it out of humanity.

4

But mysteries remain. In spite of the decrees of scientific fundamentalists, people still have experiences that reveal the soul and her enigmas. Such experiences are often very puzzling, but they still deserve our attention.

Despite the bias against soul, there are thoughtful people who take it seriously—for instance, psychologists of Jungian persuasion. Carl Gustav Jung, and the new archetypal soul doctors, have done much to revive the ancient sense of the soul's worth and depth. There are psychic forces deeper than our personal selves— forces that influence our destinies.

Besides Jung and his school, there is psychical research: the study of extrasensory perception (ESP) and psychokinesis (PK)— which also testify to mysteries of the Heraclitean soul. There are big gaps in our understanding of human personality: I am convinced the data show this. My own experiences have helped convince me.

5

When I was a student of philosophy at Columbia University, I had some strange experiences that affected my idea of soul. They involved things most of my teachers said were impossible. ESP is impossible, one of my professors said, for that would imply dualism—and dualism is impossible!

All such talk of "impossibilities" left me unmoved. My observations assured me there was much in human experience that science had barely begun to fathom. My own puzzling encounters prompted me to do further research; I read deeply into the literature of psychic phenomena, and I began to collect my own data. After fifteen years of exploring the far side of the psyche, I would say this: If we are bold enough to follow the leads from our extraordinary experiences, we may discover things in inner space as remarkable as those Galileo discovered in outer space.

6

But exploring inner space is difficult. We have yet to invent a telescope for probing the psychic galaxies. Soul data come coded in images, symbols, and curious co-incidences. To decipher the signals from the universe of soul we need special tools; imagination, for instance, is one kind of "telescope" we use to probe the outer reaches of inner space.

The problem is that since the Renaissance we typically underrate the skills required for psychic exploration. Descartes is often blamed for this. Yet a revolt against Cartesian rationalism began as early as 1709 with Giovanni Battista Vico, who rebuked Descartes for making logic the measure of all being. We understand human experience, said Vico, through *fantasia*—through the power of imagination—the master key for unlocking the soul's mysteries.

7

In this book, I use the word "psychic" to portray experiences that unlock the door to our inner depths: great dreams, psychedelic trips, paranormal episodes.

How many of us have been educated to believe we are one-dimensional beings straying aimlessly in a metaphysical flatland? Is there a way out? Can we recapture the lost dimensions of our souls?

I think there are many ways we can. In my case, for instance, certain unusual dreams stirred up feelings of tremendous inner resources. People are often guided by significant, memorable dreams. We need to learn the art of shoring up their meanings and using their healing powers.

Perhaps the most spectacular psychic events in modern history were the appearances of the Virgin Mary in Zeitun, Egypt (1968-1971). Indeed, Goddess epiphanies are being reported all over the world today, and I think they hold an important message for soulmakers. The Goddess—Jung's "anima"—points to the depths of the unconscious psyche. By opening up to the "feminine," by yielding to the unconscious, we open up to the mysteries of soul life. For example, encounters with UFOs may open us up to the mysteries; they seem, in fact, to signal, at least in many cases, the beginnings of inner transformation. For Jung, they signified a changing of the gods. Later on I describe a UFO experience that fits this pattern.

It may be awkward to admit, but in my search for the boundaries of soul, drug experiences played a part. The secrets of the soul sometimes need to be teased out, and long ago shamans discovered the virtues of psychoactive plants. Thanks to my experiments with such plants, I was able to discover important aspects of soul life.

The soul of the ancients roamed freely in time, and I want to tell of experiences that expanded my idea of time. In one, I had three "impossible" previews of the attempt on President Ronald Reagan's life in 1981. In another curio of time's antics, I "met" the amazing Swami Nadabrahmananda in a prophetic dream. Precognition deepens the mystery of soul.

The soul of the ancients was a soul that travelled beyond the body. The idea of soul travel may seem fantastic; nevertheless, people continue to report the experience. The out-of-body experience (OBE), so well documented today, again adds to the mystery of soul. In this book I report two unusual cases.

And the soul of the ancients survived bodily death—an idea out of favor with modern science. Still, people have experiences that suggest we do survive death. My experiences prove at least one thing to me: There is more to death than meets the eye.

*There may be intelligences or sparks of divinity
in millions—but they are not Souls till they acquire
identities, till each one is personally itself.*
                                                      John Keats

PART ONE
THE SOUL LOST

For us moderns the very idea of soul—the vital core of our being—is in question. But this is nothing new, for among the first people as well as among the first philosophers, owning our selves—our souls—was always a perilous achievement.

The elders of the tribe no longer teach the secrets of soul life. That's the first strike against us—we are educated to soullessness. Then there's the general wear and tear of life itself, exposure to the normal shocks of growing up, the countless episodes we barely notice that secretly rob us of inner strength. Perhaps our most subtle obstacle is the need to repress our own soul life, the fear of opening up to the terror and the beauty of existence. Finally, to complete the attack on Alice in Wonderland, there is one major storm the soulmaker must weather: the eye-opening discovery of mortality.

The magic words shall hold thee fast:
Thou shalt not heed the raving blast.

Lewis Carroll

Chapter One

The Attack on Alice in Wonderland

When I was a graduate student at Columbia University, I had a strange dream. I dreamt I was at a philosophy convention and that I had lost my head. I walked around and asked several wise-looking philosophers if there was a Lost and Found, a place where I might be able to check in and collect the head I misplaced. Much to my surprise, nobody noticed my missing appendage.

Still, it wasn't too hard to manage without my head—no pain, just a sense of uneasiness, bordering on nausea. Unfortunately, I was so busy looking for my head, I missed the lectures in the halls and rooms. I wandered among crowds of great thinkers, looking for what I guessed would be the Lost and Found Room. But to no avail.

For a long time I pondered my dream. A psychoanalyst might suspect I was suffering from castration anxiety: In the unconscious, "head" and "penis" might be equivalent in meaning. I prefer to say my "head" was a symbol of my soul. Either way, the dream didn't bode well for philosophy. For, from the viewpoint of my unconscious, philosophy had been put in the role of castrator. My education, according to my unconscious, was castrating my soul— the vital core of my being.

2

The great soul doctor, Carl Jung, wrote a book called *Modern Man in Search of a Soul.* The title implies that we have lost our souls. What does it mean to "lose soul"? Is there such a thing or is "soul" just a word, a verbal fossil, an antiquated superstition?

3

Have we moderns lost our souls? Have we been cut off from the deeper, wiser, healing part of ourselves? Many feel that we have, and more than ever people are searching for something intangible and elusive, something called soul.

America has become the melting pot where all the spiritual energies of the planet seem to be merging and giving birth to new forms of consciousness. We are in the midst of a massive soul search, and signs are everywhere of a budding psychic revolution. The atmosphere sometimes seems charged with invisible presences, thronged with mysterious messengers from what Plato called the *allos topos*—the *other place*. These unidentified and mysterious beings that invade us from we know not where—channelled guides, UFO goblins, Virgin goddesses, and innumerable others from the domain of the elf-shot—are signs of turbulence in our collective soul life.

4

What is soul? The idea is as old as the human race. The root of primitive animism, it flowered in the higher religions and appears in all idealistic philosophies. Where did the soul idea come from?

Sir Edward Tylor, the British anthropologist, tried to reconstruct its origins. Let me describe a few steps of his argument. The first people noticed a difference between a living man and a corpse. Apparently, the material substance was the same in either case; *something* therefore had to be missing. *Something* must leave the body when it dies—what else but the man's life?

This life they called his soul.

Here, the etymology of words for soul—psyche, *spiritus*, ghost, *Geist*, Atman, *prana*, *Nephesh*, *Ruach*, all meaning wind or breath—bears witness to the origin of the soul idea. The soul is the breath of life.

The first people were logical: A dead person stops breathing. Life is therefore breath. Those who have a greater portion of soul are called "inspired"—they breathe more fully. And to die, of course, is to "expire"—to blow out. Early people believed that the soul leaves the mouth at the moment of death. The soul—the vital principle—thus explained death.

The first psychologists observed the difference between a living and a dead man. But they observed something else: images of people, some known to be dead, moving evasively about in their dreams. This must have made a strong impression.

And there was something else. The first people also encountered, as we still do, ghosts, that is, waking images and phantoms of dead people. Dream images of people and phantoms of the dead thus led the first thinkers to picture the soul as an image or double or shadow.

So every person has two things: a life and a double—a separable shade or image. Now, if you combine the vital breath principle with the image or double, you have the essence of the primitive idea of soul. You have, in effect, the real person; for it's this breath-image that leaves the body at death and graduates to other worlds.

Now, once the first people saw that there were souls, they decided there must be a category of great souls. These they associated with great things. The Greeks called the earth soul Gaia and the sky soul Zeus and the sea soul Poseidon and the love soul Aphrodite. The greatest souls were gods and goddesses. And so the religions were born from the first speculations on soul life.

5

Now note the next twist in the story. If soul is a thing separable from body, if it leaves the body permanently at death, and wanders off in sleep, may it not be lost from time to time? Even more dismaying is the risk of our souls being stolen. Once we admit the possibility that our souls are stealable, an even more troublesome idea suggests itself: Alien, and perhaps malign, souls may contrive to fill the vacancy. In other words, if souls are stealable, souls are possessable.

This complicates our predicament. We might almost prefer being soulless; we would then only have to worry about protecting our bodies.

Two more ideas emerge from this story of the soul's genesis. First, the primitive idea of sickness, accident, and bad luck is associated with soul loss or soul theft. When we get sick or become unhappy or suffer misfortune, it is because of loss or injury done to our souls. The first people were strict determinists. Nothing unpleasant results from happenstance. Something or somebody has damaged, weakened, stolen, or possessed some portion of our soul-stuff. The first people knew that to deal with soul-problems you had to use soul-methods. You needed, in short, soul or psychic healers.

Hence arose the idea of the shaman.

Since we can lose our souls, there is a need for people with a gift for finding them. In my dream where I lost my soul-head, there was a shortage of shamans. No one to help me find my soul! No soul-finders, no soul-menders were available for consultation. In a

way, it was the most important thing I learned in graduate school:
I had lost my soul and nobody but myself could help me find it
again.

6

Soul life has been evolving since Neanderthal people first buried
their dead. Along the way, let us remember, soul belief has led to
many absurd notions and cruel practices. To a man of rank, it
seemed natural that servants should follow him to the next world.
Among the Fiji in the Pacific islands, for example, the high point
of a great man's funeral was strangling his wives, friends, and
slaves. Head-hunting obeyed the same logic; the soul, severed from
a foe's head, would serve the head-hunter in the next world. Ghastly
forms of soul loss and soul theft, to be sure.

"Having a soul" is an unstable state of affairs. Plato understood
the essential risk of soul loss, which nowadays we call neurosis,
depression, hopelessness, anomie, existential vacuum, and by
many other fancy names. Plato refined the concept of soul. Above
all, for Plato the soul was the organ of contact with a higher world
of Ideas or Archetypes. By means of the soul we train ourselves to
live on earth in harmony with the wisdom of higher realities.
Philosophy, as Plato conceived it, meant learning how to assume
full ownership of our souls.

7

If it was hard to own one's soul in early times, it is just as hard
today. Ideas and events crowd upon us daily, churning up consciousness, speeding cycles of change, mixing everything in a
collage of instant obsolescence and future shock. Our traditional
ideas about reality have been shattered, and it is no longer clear that
we ever *had* souls. Most educated people today doubt whether
souls possess exotic powers such as clairvoyance, prophecy or the
ability to leave the body.

In our time, the better metaphor seems to be not finding but
making our souls. We suffer from a generally weakened belief in
the reality of soul, while we also face the perennial dangers of losing
or having our souls stolen. All-too-often we are the victims of
"head-hunters" in the guise of people supposed to be helping us.

For some reason, the following memory sticks in my head.

8

One sunny spring day in junior high school, Mrs. Atkinson, my
guidance counselor, was lecturing on the virtues of tidiness. A

workman knocked on the door, and poked his head in. A shipment of books had arrived.

"Would anyone like to help this man?" asked Mrs. Atkinson.

Up shot my hand, faster than the speed of light.

"Michael!" cried Mrs. Atkinson. I leaped from my seat. Anything was better than sitting in a stuffy classroom on a bright spring day. And a lovely day it was! I passed a jolly hour helping move books around, enjoying the warm sunshine. I had a few laughs with the workman, and all in all felt pretty good about myself. I escaped class but also did a "good" deed. A rare but happy coincidence! So I sauntered back into the classroom, beaming with pride.

Mrs. Atkinson was waiting, her brow gnarled with indignation.

"Go to my closet," she said. I obeyed. "Open the door!" I opened the door. "Look at yourself in the mirror!" she snapped. Confused, I looked at myself.

"Wha'd' I do?"

"I didn't mean *you,* when I said Michael," she explained. "I meant *that* Michael!" She pointed to *another* Michael across the room—apparently a superior version of myself.

"I'd *never* call on you—to represent *our* class."

She marched up to me. "Look at yourself!" Tie in a whirl, hair messed up, shirt hanging out. (I was being forced to see myself in a poor light.) Mrs. Atkinson stood there, arms folded, jaw righteously firm. The rest of the kids, grinning uneasily, eyed me, as I crawled away—mistaken for my better.

9

There are all kinds of obstacles to the evolution of our soul life. The biggest come from deep within ourselves. We ourselves need to diminish the fullness of our soul life. This enemy inside shows itself under the many faces of fear, and the most subtle fear is the fear of life itself. A need to recoil from full contact with existence secretly dominated me for a long time.

One summer afternoon at Montauk Point I was wandering on an isolated beach, feeling wonderfully expansive in the presence of the sea and the open sky. The boundaries between myself and everything around me seemed to be melting away. Not a care in the world, not a single unpleasant thought. Happy, in perfect health. Lost in the sound of the surf, rapt by the sight of a white gull, I felt myself dissolving—like a footprint on the wave-washed shore. A feeling, beyond words, of oneness with everything.

Suddenly, I felt a pinching sensation on my back—as if someone were spying on me. I glanced up and down the shoreline. I expected to see somebody, a truant officer, a policeman, a priest in a black forbidding uniform.

But there was nobody.

I continued to feel the odd sensation, which made me contract, and become self-conscious. I forgot the sea and the sky. I couldn't shake the feeling I was being watched by a disapproving intelligence. Something was holding me back from going all the way, from fully embracing the moment, from feeling the full girth of myself.

It wasn't the first time I caught this inner saboteur tricking me out of my bliss, trapping me with false images of fear. The truth is I often caught myself resisting bliss. For a long time I lived in a state of timid reserve, my posture in the presence of being twisted from holding myself back. I was afraid of surrendering to joy as much as I was afraid of death.

10

The first book I can remember reading was Lewis Carroll's *Alice's Adventures in Wonderland.* One day this Alice of my boyish imagination met a man of science. It took some years, of course, before the auspicious event took place. I was a high school student, and my interest in science and mathematics was awakening. I found a fascinating book by Alfred Korzybski, *Science and Sanity.*

This scholarly tome cast a curious spell on my imagination. When I was a child and first read of Alice's exploits, I saw things with clarity and distinctness—not a logical but an imaginal clarity and distinctness. When Lewis Carroll wrote that Alice fell down a rabbit hole, I actually saw a little girl with green eyes and dimpled chin tumbling down a tunnel.

After Alfred, imagining Alice got harder.

For Alice, words were things. Indeed, Alice sensed that the universe was a word: the sign of a hidden intention. And so she guessed that the converse was true: that words are universes.

In the beginning was the Word—that was my credo.

The Alice in me loved the lingo of soul: folklore and fairytales, vatic runes and nursery rhymes, nonsense and epic poetry.

But in time I became more analytic, more critical. I learned, in short, to inhibit myself—a necessary part of growing up. I learned to dissect words into cold connotations. I learned to distance myself—not only from words—but from things. And, finally, from people. The influence of Korzybski—of the scientific attack on Alice in Wonderland—was striking. In time, I became de-animated, de-souled. In a word, *deader.*

11

Science and Sanity. What a fine, proud, and sober title! Yet even it started out as a magical book for me. The blue cloth cover, the pages of numbered paragraphs, the epigraphs from Max Planck, Pierre Duhem, Hans Weyle, and other wizards from the world of science. Much fine talk of the delusive power of words, the metaphysical hazards of syntax, the nervous system mesmerized by warped linguistics.

Alfred said to Alice: "The word is only a map of reality. Once we free ourselves from old maps that misdescribe the world, we can devise new ones, and use them to test the way things really are. If a map doesn't quite work, we revise it. If it's misleading, we scrap it."

Such is the way of science. And such is the way to lead the world to sanity. Alfred, who was quite large and powerful, sat Alice on his knee; his face was stern, grave, and wise. Solemnly he peered into Alice's eyes and said: "The important point, my child, is this: We must repeat to ourselves, day and night, this simple sentence, the cornerstone of science and sanity: 'The word is not the thing. The word is not the thing. The word is not the thing.' "

It might be dangerous for Alice to grow up believing that words were things. People might take advantage of her credulity. A sly man might charm her with flattery, a jewel peddlar convince her a piece of glass was a diamond, or a politician enlist her fidelity with clever slogans. Alice knew she had to quit flying about with her friend the dove, and get down on her knees, and touch the earth, and go to school with the wise serpent. So she forgot her antique Thoth, her magus and soul master, and sat at the feet of Alfred Korzybski.

12

Alice left Alfred, wiser no doubt, but her step had lost its spring, and the sky now looked a little bleaker, somewhat like the sane and scientific face of her new mentor. Her first reaction—after the flush of pride in having learned something faded—was to feel a shudder of loneliness pass through her loins.

She found, in fact, that though she had begun to collect new world maps, none of them quite seemed to fit like the old ones. Despite the new maps, she got lost whenever she went out. After a while it was no longer clear where she was going or why she was going anywhere at all. The maps multiplied, became more complicated, and her bag of them now weighed more than she did.

Alice grew weary. The sun no longer rose over the hilltop with a voice, warm and confiding. The stars and moon no longer winked at her, as if they were on holiday.

Alice had become less animated.

Then something even more disturbing happened. She became afraid of the dark. (She had no maps to guide her through the dark worlds.)

Alice was walking home during the first snowfall of the year, when three boys jumped out from behind an oak tree, and began to push her around and laugh at her. Her first impulse was to play a game with them, and make believe they were friends.

Then she remembered Alfred Korzybski's refrain. "The word is not the thing." It seemed to echo on the lonely street, and in the darkening hollow of the sky, Alice heard screams. She turned toward the boys, and realized how large they had become, and how ugly and mean their faces were. They crowded around her and whispered into her ears: "You are going to die. You are going to die. You are going to die."

It is not the universal and the regular that characterize the individual but rather the unique.

C. G. Jung

PART TWO
ROADS TO RECAPTURING THE SOUL

Each soul is unique and each soul has been wounded or lost in a unique way; therefore, each soul has to follow its own path of soulhealing and soulmaking. We take this trip alone, make our own maps and myths; there is no other way, for no one has been where we are now.

Soulmaking feeds on individual experience. If we hope to deepen our understanding of the soul and her neglected powers, we need to open ourselves to whatever hints and clues experience puts in our way. As soulmakers we make ourselves over from our experiences, like artists who play with and rearrange the raw materials of their craft. Experiences that nudge us out of the rut of everyday consciousness are roads to recapturing the soul.

The next three chapters map three distinct roads to recapturing the soul. In Chapter 2, I cover the road of great dreams. A subject that merits further study, I offer examples of my own, to show how they may help one along the path of soulmaking. This leads (in Chapter 3) to a type of experience occurring on a worldwide basis: an encounter with a figure of light believed to be the Virgin Mary. Numinous images of the goddess are appearing everywhere today and they have something important to say about soulmaking. From here we move on to a UFO encounter, another worldwide pattern of soul changing experiences.

Have you built your ship of death, O have you?
O build your ship of death, for you will need it.

D. H. Lawrence

It is no easy matter to live a life that is modelled on Christ's, but it is unspeakably harder to live one's own life as truly as Christ lived his.

C. G. Jung

Chapter Two
Great Dreams

It happened when I was a teenager. One day it struck me with abnormal clarity that I—my bodily self—was doomed, sooner or later, to die. The effect on my sense of reality was disorienting. I immediately thought: There must be a way out of this—there must be a way to escape death.

My imagination did an about face and attacked me. Out of the dark sprang fear, like a mad dog, and sank its teeth into my leg. The universe suddenly appeared like a nightmare of senseless becomings—nature like a gigantic killing factory. There was nothing physically wrong with me. The idea of my inevitable death just became intolerably clear.

Somehow the normal defenses and illusions that keep most people sealed from the dark side of existence were stripped away, and I saw straight into the Abyss—the Truth of the Dissolution of All Things. It was a terrific blow to my psyche, and I became prey to morbid ideas. Instead of my old childhood fear of the dark, the fear of another kind of darkness filled my mind—the fear of death.

2

Yet the moment these fears began to assail me, an inner consoler began to surface from within—a source of allies in the shape of haunting images from the unconscious. The awareness of death was a blow to my psyche, but that very blow opened me to a world of instructive dreams.

3

Dreams! What mysteries hide behind this plain word! Oddly enough, some academics today deny that dreams are real experiences. I find it puzzling that anyone could talk himself out of believing in dreams. I would guess that such people have weak, pale dreams, and for that reason find it easy to doubt that they are real.

For my part I believe in dreams. I know dreams that show the confetti of my mind blowing helter-skelter, after the parade of an ordinary day, and I know higher dreams that take me on voyages to exotic places at the far side of the psyche.

Call it a process of compensation. As my conscious picture of the world flattened and grayed, my dream life took on more depth and assumed more brilliant colors. Some dreams were supernormally tinted, glimpses of my self slipping through the net of time and space—fledgling psychic dreams that seemed to say that my real "I" included more than I could presently imagine.

I could fill a book with trivial examples. I recall a dream, for instance, when I was a teenager. I was playing handball with a boy on the block I hardly knew. After breakfast, I stepped outside into the street and ran into the boy I had just dreamed of. He was bouncing a ball and the first thing he said was: "How about a game of handball?"

4

Certain dreams were like snapshots of otherworldly beauty. *I'm walking under a sky bluer than any blue I ever saw through waking eyes. Impossible to describe this color of dawn skies and cloudless noontimes: this blue essence drawn from the reservoir of all blue memories.*

In the absence of sensory input, we produce these inner scenes. That we dream at all is unexplained by current brain science—that colors appear with such purity and brilliance deepens the riddle. It's as if some artificer within—a master at Plato's Academy—wants to display samples from the Heaven of Ideas.

I wonder about dreams that don't replay familiar sensations: dreams that seem to bring us back to a previous aquatic existence. I recall a dream of myself swimming in a lake, luxuriating in a sense of buoyancy, before I ever learned to swim. Somewhere deep down, a residue perhaps from life in my mother's womb, I had a clear memory of buoyancy. And what of flying dreams? Are they also replays of our days in the womb? Or avian echoes from the collective memory of life? Or are they perhaps foreshadowings of soul travel?

5

The fear of death poisoned my picture of the world. My psychic link to the vital powers of the universe was broken. Despite the dizzying reaches of space, the awesome numbers of stars and galaxies I knew were out there, I felt oddly confined, and suffered from a kind of metaphysical claustrophobia. An ancestral voice whispered of forgotten homelands, and I felt what the surrealist painter, Giorgio de Chirico, once called a *nostalgia for the infinite.*

6

I made an important discovery. Two sources were available to help me form a picture of the world. One was built of stuff garnered from the accidents of personal experience; the other came from some larger experience, from the far older, perhaps wiser memory of humankind.

I seemed to sense the presence, the operation of an intelligence from beyond the ken of my conscious mind. This other intelligence had a wider vision and scanned the universe with a surer sense of my place in it. I was drawn to this other intelligence. In those days I seemed to live my life at the night pole of my being: among the roller-coasters, penny-arcades, and winter-beaches of my dreams.

7

A back street of Coney Island. Off to the left, the towering Parachute Jump overlooks the Atlantic. A gang of angry men— thieves, beggars, lowlife—are chasing me. I turn inside a restaurant, walk down the aisle. The tables are set in white linen, the people stop eating and look up. Outside, the men are forcing their way in.

A door opens. I step in, climb a narrow spiral staircase leading to a small oval-shaped door, grab the knob and shake it violently. A hand reaches from nowhere, touching my shoulder. I look up and see a woman dressed in blue. She opens the door, and gentles me out. A green hill, drenched in golden sunlight, slopes in the distance.

8

A boy with his mother, playing at the seashore. A ship appears. A majestic woman, standing at the helm, beckons the boy to join her. He wants to, but is afraid. He can't swim. Curious, he steps into the water, is caught by a wave, and is swept toward the boat. He tries to paddle back to shore, but the woman steps into the water, lifts him up, and takes him aboard.

9

A great crowd of people on Fifth Avenue. Tremendous excite-ment, horn-blowing and flag-waving—like a circus or a parade. It is the day of the Lord. It is the day of the Second Coming. Newspaper and television people, public officials and dignitaries gather in expectation. There are believers, there are doubters, there are the merely curious.

A blast of trumpets, banners waving above the crowd. A form appears, a solitary figure, moving swiftly. It's happening—the Unprecedented. The form is vague, at first a little cloud. Now it is defining itself. I cannot recognize the figure who suddenly, boldly, turns around. An arm raised toward the crowd, toward the sky. The people roar. Cries of astonishment. It is She. The New Christ is a Woman!

10

Some dreams give clues to the pattern of our lives—perhaps to the pattern of life itself—these I call great dreams. A simple category. I think that most of us have great dreams from time to time, though when I try to describe what seems to me their main features people sometimes look a bit puzzled.

Great dreams stand out by virtue of a feeling of tremendous untapped meaning, a residue of enchantment, an afterglow that warms the memory, not just for weeks or months, but sometimes for years. We can return to our great dreams for encouragement, for precious hints of wisdom. Great dreams contain inexhaustible truths, and orient us, like runes, toward our futures. One hesitates to try to explain them; one wants to dance them, act them out in living gestures. The more we put ourselves into a great dream, the more we get back. Great dreams are wells that never run dry.

11

I was living on Sedgewick Avenue in the Bronx at the corner where Kingsbridge Road dips downward toward the Hudson river. It was August, 1968. I was working on my doctoral dissertation, *Plato and the Myth of the True Earth.* I went to sleep early that night—about ten o'clock.

Soon after falling asleep, I woke up sweating. There was a strange light above me, in the corner of the ceiling—a smoldering orange glow. Several times a soft globule of colored light appeared in my room. A light that feels alien yet curiously familiar. I drifted, sensing the orange glow, flickering, filling the room with a queer uneasy presence.

I come to a dark doorway where people are gathered. Something in the doorway is attracting them. For a moment I'm afraid to look. I notice a dull light flicker—like the glow I saw in my bedroom before I fell asleep.

The people laugh; they say it's a trick.

I keep looking. One by one, the people in the street walk away—except for a woman wearing a habit. A nun whose face is hidden.

She remains by the door, beckoning me to look inside. It seems easy now. All fear is gone, and I look more closely. Down through a dark corridor, as if at a great distance, I see the figure of Christ. A painful writhing in my chest, I start to sweat as it comes into focus. He looks weary and walks slowly; his robes are tattered.

A woman holds him by the arm. They move as in a slow dance, in a halo of soft timeless light. There is a third person, an important figure, identity unknown. They pass on and disappear into the dark.

The nun lays her hand on my arm, as if to reassure me. Now the doorway begins to change. I am watching Christ again, bright and vivid on a giant screen. Something odd now. The Savior has a long braid and two fangs. Even so, he is beautiful, and familiar, like the face of Bellini's Christ. But also alien, synthetic, and vaguely satanic.

12

A great dream about the duplicity of Christ. There is a Christ who appears through the doorway of soul, a Christ wed to the female. The whole Christ, the Christ within, the psychic Christ born from the sweat and struggle of inner life.

There is also a synthetic Christ, a show Christ, beautiful, brilliant—with fangs. A consumer, a TV personality, an image produced by a machine. You can turn it on and off at will—a fake giant TV Christ.

13

Something about staginess, acting, role-playing. A quiet caveat against syncretism. You cannot make a true and whole soul out of the rags and tatters of alien cultures. You cannot piece your victory together out of other people's spiritual conquests. It has to be your own battle, your own unique living synthesis.

Over and over I got this image: An element of flim-flam, ambiguity, uncertainty is built into the job of becoming a complete human being. There is no settling into pure verity, untainted by doubtful shadows. Perhaps the angels perceive truth with unwavering perfection, but for us humans, us creatures of the humus, the precious stones of truth are always mixed with a little dung.

14
My dreams were pulling me toward the dark unconscious, urging me to set sail on the great waters of death, prodding me to be like a female, open and yielding to the forces stirring within myself. About this time I had a great dream that took me deeper than my Christian cultural unconscious. Still alive in my memory, this dream brought me back to the dawn of history and the symbols of ancient Egypt—back to a mysterious light and energy that quickened my soul life.

15
Crowds of people have committed unspecified crimes. They are preparing to escape to a forbidden land. I walk among them, uncertain of my allegiance. A man emerges from the crowd—a German who proclaims himself a leader. He shows us an odd structure, a vehicle with a motor; but some are doubtful. The man exudes confidence; he says he was once a general.

We need wood to build a ship for our journey. The old general leads us to a strange place. A spacious garden, inside a glass-covered hothouse. Inside the hothouse, a glider, a flying ship. Our mission, to find wood.

And inside the garden a catacomb, filled with tombs, wooden coffins. The coffins are very old. We decide to open one and break it in pieces for the wood. It belongs to George Washington. I expect to see something ghastly. Instead, within the coffin is another coffin, and within that another, and so on. I peel off layer upon layer, and with each layer the wood changes into something reddish, leathery. Something alive.

A bright red-purplish beetle with thin delicate wings.

The general calls me. There is something I have to help move. Is it a coffin? Or is it a glider? I start to haul this thing up a hill.

Up, up the hill I haul. As I haul this glider-coffin, the sun rises over the hill. The sun is marvelously bright. Its rays penetrate my heart, filling me with sublime, indescribable bliss. A friend, a painter, is walking beside me. We notice the red beetle hopping away. I to him: "It's good to know one sees the sun again." And he: "Yes, one gets to see the sun many times."

16
The radiant joy I felt in this dream has remained with me for over twenty years. Few events in my outer life have made such an

impression. A memory of waves of bliss streaming from the sun, flooding my heart while I was hauling what looked like my coffin up a hill.

Later in the 1970s, I discovered the new research on the near-death experience. The symbolic coupling of light and death in my dream was reinforced by this work. The more I read accounts of these near-death encounters, the more I felt they were about a place I had been to. I had seen and felt that light myself. The encounter was brief, but it burnt its way into my soul forever.

In my death dream, I seemed to come face to face with what near-death researcher Raymond Moody has called the Being of Light. The fact that I was not literally near death, but dreaming, seemed significant. I felt I was given an inside clue to the nature of this Being of Light.

The light I experienced wasn't restricted to near-death experiences. I found there was a family of experiences similar to the near-death experience. I wondered if I'd struck a deep vein in the collective unconscious, a pattern of psychic imagery and energies tied to death and dying. I dubbed this pattern the Archetype of Death and Enlightenment, and came to think it was a clue to the evolution of human consciousness. I put my observations and speculations in a book (*The Final Choice*, Stillpoint, 1985).

17

I had no knowledge at the time of Ra, the Sacred Scarab, or other items in Egyptian symbolism and mythology. The detail about coffins within coffins, which was part of an ancient Egyptian burial custom, I found in Sir Wallace Budge's books years later. Somehow one of the oldest myths of the world, far from my conscious awareness, came to life in my own consciousness.

18

And yet this isn't quite so surprising. I—all of us—have to take the same journey Osiris took three thousand years before Christ: the journey through dismemberment to resurrection, through soul loss to soulmaking.

What the ancient Egyptians knew, the wise teacher within knows: To reach the sun of soul consciousness, we have to cross the sea of death. And to cross the sea of death, we have to build a ship. We have to build a "ship of death," to use a phrase from a great poem by D. H. Lawrence.

My dream was about building a ship. About the "ship" we have to build to cross the sea of death—the ship of soul. Ship-builder, soulmaker, I have to build my own ship, I have to make my own soul. Get the material anyway I can—ransack the high and the mighty—I've got build my own soulcraft.

19

I call this a great dream because I can still drink from the fountain of its many meanings. It took me to the place where I saw the light of love's being, touching a source of bliss. And it promised I could return there again and again.

The picture of death painted by my educated, conscious mind contrasted sharply with the picture painted by the artist of the deep unconscious—a picture for soulmakers to contemplate: Death as the port to Eternity's Sunrise.

I am nature, the Universal mother, mistress
of all the elements, primordial child of time,
sovereign of all things spiritual, queen of the
dead, queen also of the immortals, the single
manifestation of all gods and goddesses.
Isis Apuleius

Chapter Three
The Lady of Light

My dreams of healing light, of the Second Goddess Coming, of Egypt and immortality were, as I look back, related to other psychic phenomena occurring in many parts of the world at the time.

Great dreams are a powerful incentive to soulmaking, but sometimes dreams aren't enough, and we need to be yanked more forcibly from our de-animated, robotic existence, by things so odd or so awesome that they stop us dead in our tracks. Our worldviews have become so hardened, so sealed to the mystery of being, that we need to be confounded by miracles. It almost seems as if some impish Mind Out There likes to shock and surprise us, as if it wants to disarm our arrogant intellects.

Shocking to reason is the twentieth century epidemic of Mary visions. One spectacular example—unnoticed in the Western world—were the phenomena of Zeitun, Egypt, which began on April 2, 1968.

2

Zeitun is located near Cairo, a busy suburb bordering what was once Heliopolis—the ancient City of the Sun. Around twilight, 8:30 P.M., at the intersection of Tumanbey Street and Khalil Lane, Moslem workmen were changing shifts at the garage of the Public Transit System. Across the street stood St. Mary's and her lofty domes, a Coptic Orthodox Christian Church.

Several workmen and pedestrians noticed something moving on the middle dome. They looked up and saw a young lady in white kneeling by the cross on the dome. One workmen, Farouk Mohammed Atwa, a Moslem, thought she was about to commit suicide.

He cried out to her, "Lady, don't jump! Don't jump!"

Then the lady stood up. She was seen wearing a bright gown of light.

One of the witnesses, a woman, shouted: "Zagharuta!" (A cry of joy.) Then she yelled: "*Settena Mariam!*" meaning, "Our Lady, Mary!"

Someone ran to summon a priest. Farouk Atwa, believing the figure was about to jump, dashed off to notify the rescue squad. Then the lady vanished.

The hand that Farouk Atwa raised while shouting at the "lady in white" was bandaged; one of his fingers, infected with gangrene, was scheduled to be amputated. The next day the surgeon was astonished to find no trace of gangrene; this was the first recorded healing of Zeitun.

3

A week later the lady appeared again, and after that several times a week. Huge crowds of Christians, Moslems, police, press, government officials and nonbelievers witnessed appearances of what came to be called a "Lady of Light."

On April 13, 1968, a photographer, Wagih Rizk Matta captured the vision on film for the first time. Most people were immobilized during the experience, unable to operate their cameras.

Said Mr. Matta: "The first time I saw the apparition, the light cloud of the Virgin Mary was so bright that it blinded my eyes. I was shaking as if I was electrified. The following two evenings similar things happened to me, but then on 13 April when the apparition was moving for ten minutes above the church, I was able to snap the camera twice. It was an awesome experience. I had the feeling that the earth below my feet would disappear."

After taking the photograph, Mr. Matta, his arm partially crippled from a car accident, healed instantly. An official medical committee, set up by the church, investigated the reported healings.

4

From April, 1968, to the early months of 1971, St. Mary's Church was the scene of aerial wonders of unearthly splendor. Thousands, possibly millions, of people saw a dazzling goddess-like form, taken by all to be the Virgin Mary. In the language of Greek Orthodoxy, Mary is *theotokos*—the God Bearer.

The Coptic Christians of this region have long expected the return of the Virgin. According to scripture, the Holy Family fled from King Herod to Egypt. The angel of the Lord appeared to Joseph in a dream and said: "Arise, and take the young child and his mother, and flee into Egypt" (MA. 2:13.).

Zeitun was one of the places where Mary, Joseph and the young child stopped and rested. Not far from Zeitun is a place called Mataria, where you can still see a very old sycamore tree, said to be the same tree Mary rested under two millennia ago.

Several people told me the story of the tree in Mataria. In 1956, city officials decided to cut down the ancient sycamore, which had been kept alive for centuries, but which had become a nuisance to traffic and business. Two city officials were sent to cut it down. When the first man raised his axe, his arms froze. When the second man struck the tree with his ax, the tree spurted blood. The two men never finished the job; the tree is still standing today.

5

The most remarkable appearances were in the early months of 1968. (Right before the assassination of Martin Luther King, Jr. and Robert Kennedy.) In April, May, and June, they occurred almost nightly; the appearances lasted from a few seconds to six hours. Unusually long appearances were reported on May 4th, 5th, and June 8th and 9th. Often there were multiple appearances in an hour. Toward 1969 they occurred at the rate of twice a week. By late 1970 and early 1971, the appearances had dwindled to about once a month, the last ones occurring in early 1971.

At Zeitun *millions* of eye-witnesses sighted a scientifically inexplicable being of light—an entity best described as an archetypal goddess-form. Sometimes she appeared half-formed, her bust alone being visible. She appeared in silhouette and was described as statuesque—a luminous statue. Sometimes, the whole form appeared. She appeared life-size, in miniature, and larger than life. At all times a being of light, a light so brilliant her features were barely distinguishable. Everyone said she looked young and beautiful.

In her presence the cross and church domes lit up. Her colors changed, and mostly she came, to use Shelley's phrase, "stained in the white radiance of eternity." Sometimes this white radiance turned golden or sapphire. Explosions of light often preceded her appearance. A luminous cloud would descend from an opening in the sky and assume her form. She vanished suddenly or faded slowly. The Lady of Light always appeared at night, twilight, or sunrise.

She walked on or hovered near the domes of St. Mary's, floated in the sky and in the courtyard by the palm trees. She appeared motionless or walked to and fro, displaying herself to the entranced multitude. She wore a luminous gown, and a crown of jewels that radiated dazzling sparks. Her gown and veils fluttered gently, as if she were hovering on a mild breeze.

Assuming an attitude of prayer, she kneeled and pointed to the cross on the dome; she bowed, waved, and blessed the crowd. One man I spoke to in Astoria, New York, a Coptic immigrant from Cairo, told me how he witnessed "the Lady in White." He had gone to her and pleaded for his sick wife. He shouted and screamed, and the Lady gestured to him, as if to say: *Calm down! You're wife is okay!* As it turned out, his wife was freed of her heart problem after he witnessed the apparition. Later, I received confirmation of this from the woman's physician.

In some appearances, the Lady of Light held what looked like the infant Jesus on her left arm; in others, she waved an olive branch, the symbol of peace. The crowds sometimes saw her as part of a tableau of the Holy Family. At other times she looked sad. At all times she was silent.

6

There were other extraordinary phenomena. Often, as a prelude to the Virgin's arrival, witnesses saw strange birds of light. (I have some intriguing photographs of these.) They look like doves or pigeons, larger than their natural counterparts, made of a brilliant light substance. They flashed above the domes, often in formations resembling crosses; they flew over the domes at extraordinary speeds, abruptly vanishing. The wings of these light-birds didn't move.

Starlike patterns of light also appeared, moved, and glowed in the sky. Brilliant blobs of light flashed at random; shafts of light blazed on the domes. The light seemed one substance; only the forms varied.

The atmosphere around the church was charged with a mysterious energy. People watched the sky turn deep red. Red clouds of fragrant incense rolled out of the church dome windows and drifted down on the crowds, further bewildering and amazing them.

7

In my view, the objective reality of the appearances is hard to repudiate. It is unlikely that they were a mass hallucination. Far too many witnesses observed essentially the same thing —indeed, millions! A quarter million people assembled by St. Mary's on certain nights, especially in the first months of the appearances.

Jammed together, shoulder to shoulder, chanting, praying, singing in Greek, in Arabic—from the Bible, the Koran—people of all ages, belief-systems, cultures: They were responding to something objective—to something "out there." Hallucinations are not so long-lasting: The appearances went on for *thirty months.*

Some said it was a CIA trick, others a light show from a Russian telstar. Government authorities, however, found no evidence of trickery, conspiracy, or deception. The Director of General Information and Complaints Department reported to His Excellency the Minister, Dr. Hafez Ghanem, that investigations showed no evidence of fraud. The report states:

"The official investigations have been carried out with the result that it has been considered an undeniable fact that the Blessed Virgin Mary has been appearing on the Coptic Orthodox Church at Zeitun in a clear and bright luminous body, seen by all present in front of the church, whether Christian or Moslem."

8

Many high officials in the Egyptian Government, including, it is said, Abdul Nasser, witnessed these prodigies. The government statements carry weight; Christians are a minority in Egypt, and Moslems would be loath to support Christian miracles. Nevertheless, the government and the Moslem community verified the visions.

Few overseas news agencies paid much attention; there was a short notice in the New York Times on May 5th, 1968. There were headlines in all six Cairo newspapers: statements issued by Coptic Pope Kyrillos VI and confirmations from Coptic clergymen. People healed by the visions appeared on television.

The special Coptic committee wrote a report on their investigation:

"We then determined to witness the blessed apparition with our own eyes, in order to have the matter cleared up plainly and evidently. We stayed opposite to the domes, watching for some nights until we could see the Blessed Virgin Mary appearing inside a luminous circle. Then she appeared in her complete form, moving on the domes, then bowing before the cross and at the end, she blessed the multitudes. Another night, we saw doves with the bright color of silver and with light radiating from them. The doves flew from the dome to the sky direct. We then glorified Almighty God who has allowed the terrestrials to see the glory of the celestials."

Pope Kyrillos' official statement: "The appearances have been witnessed by many thousands of citizens and foreigners belonging to different religions and sects, together with groups of religious organizations and scientific and professional personages and all other categories of people, . . .confirming the certainty of the

Virgin's appearances—all giving the same particulars as to description and form and time and place, thus proving . . . the matter of appearance above any doubt or any lack of proof or evidence."

The appearances were photographed. This would seem to imply some measure of physical objectivity. The photographs and their negatives have been carefully studied; no evidence of tampering or anything fraudulent has been found. The photographs I have seen, taken by Mr. Matta, show clearly defined forms of the archetypal virgin figure (as well as large fat pigeon-like creatures scurrying across the sky); some of his photos reveal half-formed blobs of light. The camera, in fact, seems to have detected a physical manifestation in various stages of materialization.

Now, to add to the confusion: Not everyone present saw the apparitions. I spoke to a woman who spent many nights at the scene of the sightings and saw nothing at all, even while crowds of souls were gazing in rapture at the Lady.

This raises a curious point. The apparitions were at least partly physical, for they affected film; but at the same time they were invisible to *some* witnesses. What sort of an object is physical only part of the time and for some of the people? The visions seem designed to melt our dualistic mindsets. The sharp contrast of real versus imaginary, objective versus subjective, physical versus mental doesn't seem to apply here. Neither does the contrast of formal and formless. The Lady of Light embraces all these opposites.

9

The impact on witnesses was tremendous. Reports of extraordinary healings were documented by a medical committee set up by the Coptic Orthodox Church.

Witnesses reported being stunned, stupefied, immobilized; riveted by the spectacle, they swayed en masse. A strange paralysis of limbs overcame many and many lost the ability to use their cameras. (Also reported in UFO encounters.) Once during an appearance of the Lady, an angry Moslem policeman started to mount a stairway to one of the Church domes. He wanted badly to expose what he thought was a trick. Just as he reached the top of the stairway leading to the dome, he was struck by a beam of light and paralyzed from the waist down; Pope Kyrillos had to pray over him before he was restored.

10

The Lady of Light always appeared silent—beyond creeds. She held up an olive branch—as the Buddha held up a flower in his last message to the world.

Has the "Second Coming" already begun? People are reporting Marian visions from all parts of the world: Medjugorje, Yugoslavia; Akito, Japan; Kibeho, Africa; Lubbock, Texas; Balinspittle, Ireland; San Daminao, Italy; Cuapa, Nicaragua; Hrushiv in the Ukraine—to give a few examples. In my dream of the Second Coming, Christ returns as a woman. People who picture the Lord returning in the guise of a flaming male superego are ignoring the signs. The signs indicate a changing of the gods—a challenge to the vitals of Western civilization.

*Only something overwhelming, no matter
what form of expression it uses, can challenge
the whole man and force him to react as a
whole.*

C. G. Jung

Chapter Four

Close Encounter of
the Jazz Kind

By 1971 visions of the Lady of Light in Egypt were on the
wane. But it was not the end of stories of strange aerial phenomena.
Some Enigma Agency that liked to display itself and confound the
rational mind was still migrating over skies elsewhere. The Cosmic
Light Show was by no means over.

Indeed, strange things have been appearing in the skies for
centuries—nowadays we call them UFOs. The modern wave of
Unidentified Flying Objects began in 1947, at the dawn of the
Atomic Age. At that time UFO sightings often centered around
military installations. It does seem, in fact, that since the birth of
the Bomb, psychic phenomena all over the world have increased.
Many believe that visitors from outer space are here to guide us
through our current planetary crisis.

UFOs and visions of the Blessed Virgin Mary seem dissimilar
enough, yet UFO mavens like John Keel and Jacques Vallee have
noted the overlap in their mysterious antics. UFOs and the Virgin
were mixed up together in Fatima on October 13, 1917.

Three Portuguese children sighted what they took to be the
Virgin Mary. On that day, thousands saw the "sun" spin on its axis,
and drop from the sky in a falling-leaf motion, flashing colored
lights and giving off heat like UFOs often do. Similar UFO-like
effects have been observed since 1981 in the small mountain town
of Medjugorje, in Yugoslavia, where there are reports of youngsters
seeing the Virgin Mary. UFOs and Marian Visions are part of a
family of unexplained sky appearances.

2

It was five days before my doctoral defense at Columbia University. I was renting a loft on Waverley street in New York, two flights above a bookstore specializing in esoteric lore. For years my treasure-trove of forbidden knowledge, Weiser's Bookstore was the Shadow—in Jung's sense—cast by the Campus of Columbia University.

I was using the loft to paint. I needed a refuge from the abstractions of academic philosophy. My teachers were experts at chopping the world up into bits and pieces, tidy doles of logic. Atoms, not organs, of meaning. Intuition—the eye of the soul—had little place in academic philosophy. I needed to integrate myself; philosophy seemed more like a tool for hastening my disintegration.

So out came the brushes, the paints, the canvas—to exercise the neglected half of my brain, the part consigned to an inferior status. Flooded by powerful and often disturbing dreams, I tried to give form, in whatever way I could, to the images of my inner landscape.

My loft on Waverley used to belong to Ad Reinhardt. Reinhardt was an American original, like Ambrose Beirce or Charles Fort. Radical minimalist, Zen painter of the dark night of the soul, Ad Reinhardt raged against everything false in art, and in the end, in his attempt to save art from trumpery, dropped the visible from visual art. Ad's thing was to paint black paintings.

Ad's black paintings were like Heidegger announcing the death of metaphysics or Cage declaring that noise was music. Reinhardt's art invited you to discern the indiscernible and visualize the invisible. Art here reached a limit—a point where it was about to mutate.

3

I lived on the top floor of 14 Bedford Street in the West Village—a cheerful, sunny apartment with windows on all sides.

April 23, 1971. 11:30 P.M.

It was a friend's birthday (Shakespeare's too, by the way). We were listening to a jazz piece by John Coltrane, *The Father and the Son and the Holy Ghost.*

Jane is sprawled on the sofa. I walk to the window facing Downing Street, lean my elbow on the top-rim of the lower window, and gaze vacantly into the clear evening sky. I'm in a mild revery from Coltrane's hypnotic beat, softly thumping my foot, slightly swaying to the rhythms of the music.

Suddenly, a cluster of dazzling white lights appears out of nowhere. The lights are larger and more brilliant than any star. They are attached to nothing I can see. They perform zigzag aerial acrobatics, it seems, in tune with Coltrane's music. Their appearance in the sky is so sudden and so silent, it takes a few seconds to realize that what I'm looking at is *very* odd. I keep listening to the music, watching the light-dance. After about twenty seconds, I realize what I'm seeing is very strange indeed.

My attention was fixed on the light-cluster flying zanily about; I yell to Jane to come to the window. She gives a start—I'm not just "seeing" things. Jane puts on her glasses, and raises the window. It's no reflection. Something is really out there! Brighter, more dazzling than any star.

The light-entity suddenly stops its aerial capers and slowly glides downward, in a straight line, toward the dome of Our Lady of Pompeii. The oldest church in Greenwich Village—built last century to serve migrants and refugees—at the corner of Carmine and Bleeker.

The lights hover there, pulsing—motionless above the cross. An unusual sensation comes over me as I stare at the strange lights in the sky: It feels as though I am flying far out into space. I am surrounded by tiny dots of distant stars. Far out among them I see the dome of Our Lady of Pompeii; the UFO lights are still pulsing above the cross.

Then I find I am back in my body. The church is just a few blocks away! But now something else. It's there, up in the sky, like a phantom! Over the lights, I see—but this more inwardly than outwardly—two large heads and massive shoulders. They look *excited!* They're *watching us!*

I recall one of the heads. It was human. I get an impression of curiosity, a kind of playful agitation. A strong feeling that I—and Jane who was half-dressed—are the objects of something distinctly *voyeuristic.*

Suddenly, the impression of the two heads fades. My attention is again riveted on the church dome. The light-cluster, above the cross, still pulsing, suddenly shoots back to where we first saw it, directly in front of the window, about two or three hundred feet above the rooftop.

Again it makes zany and "impossible" aerial maneuvers. Then, without warning, it hop-flies beetle-like across the skyline, going North. We observe its trajectory, scramble to the other window, and watch it take one last curving leap over the top of the Empire State Building—where it *vanishes.*

4

For a moment, Jane and I stood by the window, staring speech-lessly into space. Then we opened the door and walked one flight up to the roof. Louie, a friend who lived downstairs, greeted us with hands outstretched, as if he wanted to grab on to something solid. Amazement was written on his face.

"Didja see it?"

A burly teenager, Louie described the lights as he saw them darting about in the sky. According to him, they were shaped like a *pyramid.* They passed directly over the rooftop, shedding a brilliant ray on him as they passed.

"Scary," he said.

Whatever it was, it made no noise. So a third person also witnessed the phenomenon.

5

What on earth was it? Swamp gas over Greenwich village? Ball lightning? Experimental secret aircraft playing games over our Lady of Pompeii? Illusion? Hallucination?

One thing we quickly ruled out was the possibility that there was some kind of light-show taking place in the neighborhood. We surely would have known of such a show. It wouldn't have taken place at 11:30 at night. Nor would it have shot beams all the way to 34th Street where we saw it disappear over the Empire State Building. And it wasn't a projected beam of light that passed over Louie's head and terrified him. In fact, there was no *beam* at all.

The first thing that struck me was the way it moved, so erratically it boggled my mind! If there weren't two other witnesses, I might have just doubted my senses, and chalked the sighting off as a weird hallucination. And the speed was astonishing! The way it changed direction was incredible. Later, when I delved into the literature of UFOs, I found that incredible zigzag movements with sudden accelerations, often from a stationary position (as when the lights shot from the cross), were *typical* of many UFO reports.

No human organism could survive such accelerations or direction changes. That much seemed certain. There was something about the whole thing I couldn't—and still can't—quite put my finger on. It is as if I almost know what it was—as though it already has, or wants to, give its secret away. The truly puzzling thing is the way the pattern of lights seemed related to its guiding intelligence. It looked to me as if this entity—whatever its ultimate nature—moved in a way that was more organic than mechanical. What we saw appeared to fly with the swiftness of thought itself.

It was as if thought itself, in some psychokinetic fashion, was causing the light movements. It was as if we had actually *watched a thought!*

But what was it? If it was thoughtlike, who or what was the thinker? All I can say with confidence is this: I believe that what we saw was either some visual projection caused by an intelligent being not physically present or something even stranger, a mental organism of unknown type.

No less difficult to explain was this. Jane and I are listening to a piece of music with the odd title: *The Father and the Son and the Holy Ghost.* Suddenly a UFO appears outside our window. As if conscious of what we're listening to, it stops its antics in the sky and hovers over Our Lady of Pompeii—it behaves as if aware of what we are doing.

And it makes a gesture to communicate.

"We know you're listening to that religious piece by Coltrane; here we are on top of the cross to prove it!" it seemed to be saying.

I am willing to consider that Jane and I had a shared hallucination. Given that we were in a perfectly normal state of mind, it's hard to imagine what set it off. But the fact that Louie, who was on the roof, also saw the same thing, makes the idea of hallucination seem very unlikely.

A point about Louie, possibly a clue to the mystery. Louie was an amateur drummer, and I'd recently told him about John Coltrane. Louie had just bought his first Trane album. A common interest in the great jazz musician might have created a psychic thread between us. But would it have been enough to cause a collective hallucination? Not very likely, in my view. And yet the subtle psychic link—little more than a common interest—*may* have made us, as a trio, receptive to the uncanny visitor.

6

At first we were bewildered. We talked of reporting it to the police, but figured nobody would believe us. I felt like keeping the incident to myself for a different reason. The experience had a feeling of privateness, as though the appearance was meant for me, and for me alone. It was, in fact, tinged with a sense of the sacred. I needed time to ruminate on what it might mean.

A landmark in the evolution of my musings on reality, I believe those lights were signs of some unknown intelligence at large.

I wish I could be more precise.

Then there was the odd web of synchronicities. About to graduate Columbia, was something making fun of me?

"Ha! Ha! Doctor, explain this!" it seemed to say. "Wise? Or ignorant of great mysteries?

Had Socrates' stingray stung me? Was I being reminded that wisdom had something to do with becoming conscious of what I didn't know?

7

There is a myth in Plato's *Phaedo* that says that this earth we dwell on is sunk in a mist-covered hollow of the True or Whole Earth. If, Plato tells us, we could educate our souls and lift ourselves from this hollow of delusion—he called it a cave in the *Republic* — we would discover an altogether different earth. This, according to Plato, is the role of philosophy, to lead us from the false to the true and whole earth. It would be an Earth, Plato said, in which everything was luminous with gemlike beauty, where perfect justice reigned and perfect health was enjoyed, and where men and women communed with the immortals face to face.

8

The UFO experience made me think a great deal about Plato's True Earth. It made me think about the education of my soul.

Were those Dionysian star-dancers above Our Lady of Pompeii harbingers of coming global changes? In Jung's view, that's what UFOs are all about: Stirrings in the living archetypes of the collective unconscious, UFOs are appearing because the old gods and goddesses, the old forms of the human spirit, are in the throes of transformation.

What we saw signalled us from the dome of Our Lady of Pompeii as we listened to *The Father and the Son and the Holy Ghost*. Extraterrestrial high science, projection of the collective unconscious, or visitor from an unknown world, it chose to appear above Our Lady of Pompeii. And Louie saw a pyramid, linking it back to Egypt, to Zeitun where the Lady of Light was making her last appearances.

9

After talking with Louie, Jane and I went back inside the apartment. The living room from which we observed the UFO seemed electrified; a high-energy presence was in the room with us. It made my body taut with excitement, and I felt like dancing or running wild.

"It felt like we were the three Magi," I said.

Jane, never effusive, just looked stunned. She said nothing at all; but her eyes were shining strangely.

I repeated my remark about the Magi.

"Yes," Jane said, not looking at me.

The Magi. My thoughts raced. We had seen the star leading to the New Bethlehem. But what sort of New Christ did this strange star portend? What sort of New Age? The star pointed to Our Lady of Pompeii—the God-Bearing Goddess.

Would the new savior be a woman? Again, I recollect my great dream of Christ the Woman. Would the new Goddess Savior like jazz? Were we watching the rising signs of a new cult of Orpheus? Orpheus the musician—like Mary—was a bestower of peace. Would Christ the Woman from Outer Space be a musician? Would she teach us a universal language of peace? A cosmic language of dance and music? Of divine play? Would the New Being improvise on the theme of the Father and the Son and the Holy Ghost? What harp would she pluck, what horn would she blow? Or were *we* perhaps the instruments she means to play upon?

10

I left the apartment in Greenwich Village, and Jane went home to Sheboygan, Wisconsin. Once in a while I'd bump into Louie around Father Demo Square, near Our Lady of Pompeii.

"Seen any lights in the sky lately," we always ask each other.

11

Myriads of humans have seen mysterious lights in the sky. Many claim telepathic contact with beings from other worlds. Many say they've been abducted and medically examined by humanoids. Still others report meeting supermen, dwarfs and assorted monsters from outer space.

Is the collective imagination going mad or are we really on the brink of wonderful—and terrifying—discoveries? Is it all a gigantic delusion or are we about to graduate to a new vision of reality?

Something is making us ask questions like these. We ask but so far there are no definite answers. It attacks our metaphysical nerves, giving us the jitters, making us stumble in the very language we use to name the "real" and the "unreal."

Imagination or reality? Fact or fiction? The effect of these experiences is to undermine that complacent distinction. They make us wonder whether there is a region of being where reality is imagination and imagination reality.

I left the loft on Waverly Place, and quit painting. A step beyond Ad Reinhardt, I had found a new kind of artwork—a surreal lightshow on the canvas of the night sky.

The question remains: Who was the Artist?

The mind was primarily concerned, not with measures and locations, but with being and meaning.

Aldous Huxley
The Doors of Perception

PART THREE
DRUGS AND THE SOUL

A good soulmaker makes use of all the leads, the hints, the gifts that nature has to offer. Nature, for instance, is generous with plants that liberate soul life. Although scholars have studied sacred plants in shamanism and ancient religions, the history of drugs and the soul has yet to be written. My education coincided with what has been called the psychedelic revolution. In my student days at Columbia University, I was surrounded by freelance explorers into what Aldous Huxley once called Mind at Large. The complexion of things has changed nowadays. The demonic side of drugs seems to have taken over. The worst nightmares about drug abuse are coming true. All higher powers have two sides. The soul herself is two-faced, and in her depths we find dancing lights and fearsome shadows; beacons of hope and reefs of fear; the smile of Christ and the sneer of Satan.

I think I am in hell; therefore I am there.
Arthur Rimbaud

Chapter Five
The Soul-Magnifying Glass

I t would be dishonest to leave it out; mind altering plants have played a role in the education of my soul. They have, in fact, played a role in educating the soul of the human race. Siberian shaman, Chinese sage, Hindu rishi, Greek mystic—all users of sacred plants that unlock the depths of the soul. All users of soul-magnifying glasses.

"Psychedelic" is an interesting word. In Greek it literally means soul clarifying. It occurs in a Platonic dialogue on power, the *Gorgias,* where it is used to describe what happens to souls at death. Death, said Socrates, clarifies the soul; it reveals the hidden corruption, the secret deeds of unjust men who in life hid behind rank and prestige; it also reveals the beauties and virtues of just souls. Death, in short, is the ultimate "psychedelic."

2
Marijuana is a plant whose female buds produce a psychoactive resin. The genesis of this substance is curious. The buds exude a protective resin, a response to the heat of the sun. The more the sun beats down on the plant, the more the tender female buds put on their self-shielding coat. That coat, ingested into the bloodstream of humans, enters the brain and alters the character of consciousness. Who could predict such a sequence of cause and effect? Marijuana puts the soul under a magnifying glass. Nothing is added, except that when the space between the fine grains becomes visible, you may be startled by what you see.

3
The topic of "drugs" is forever in the news. It is not always treated with sterling candor. Countless Americans use mind-chang-

ing drugs, causing death and misery for thousands and costing billions of dollars. Among the worse offenders are alcohol and tobacco, known killer drugs, and all legal.

You also have illegal mind-changers, as costly in dollars and suffering. Despite the catastrophic consequences, people keep using drugs. The widespread drive to use mind-altering substances—even when it's against the law or involves the risk of death—is a remarkable fact. What are we to make of it?

The universal use of drugs, legal and illegal, says something about us; in my view, it signifies revulsion against the way the world is routinely experienced. At the core of this revulsion is metaphysical discontent. People who want to change their consciousness are people who want to change their reality. The drug problem is thus a problem of practical metaphysics.

If so many people use drugs, it is because of some need. To deal with drugs we have to deal with that need. But first we have to understand the nature of the need. Some people use drugs because their everyday life is intolerable; they need to blunt the edge of a reality that's ugly, boring, oppressive. Other people use drugs for "recreation"—a word that suggests a superficial and desacralized activity, a playful diversion from "serious" reality.

In my opinion, there is an instinct to modify the inner environment, whether it be to improve one that is poor or to explore an altogether new one. It doesn't matter what the quality of life is or at what level of society we find ourselves: People will *invent* reasons for using mind altering substances.

I am so convinced of this, I am ready to declare it a drive impelling our psychic evolution: The drive to modify the inner environment, it is as basic as the drive for sex, food, shelter.

This drive to refurbish the inner environment, to explore the heights and depths of consciousness, seems closely related to our religious impulses. It reflects an experimental curiosity in the human animal, a natural love of transcendent adventures. The failure to understand this drive, which is less about drugs than about the evolution of soul, is exacting a terrible cost.

The drug crisis signals an evolutionary crisis. Everywhere are signs of a fatal instability in human consciousness. The trouble is that nobody has the slightest idea of what to do about it. Moralizers moralize and politicians periodically jump on the bandwagon and declare "war" on drugs.

But consider this metaphor. How do we fight a "war" against a basic drive of consciousness? How do we stamp out a fundamental discontent, a fundamental restlessness in the human soul itself?

4

It was my duty to try marijuana, Bloom told me, a fellow graduate student back in the Sixties. What? Me! The Killer Weed! I had Bach's music, Van Gogh's paintings, Whitman's poetry to space me out.

One rainy Saturday night I decided to do my duty. My maiden voyage into Mind at Large. We were sitting around Bloom's hellhole apartment on Riverside Drive when the rolling papers and plastic weed bag appeared. Bloom rolled as he talked. Not bothering to clean out seeds or twigs, he licked and re-licked cheap, ungummed papers, piling up joints, his face animated at the prospect of an all-night symposium on all and nothing. Bloom's energy, the headlong stream of his rap, the tidbits of Hegel, Marx, Marcuse peppered with hipster phrasings, got to me.

At first I hesitated. In my mind the weed carried unsavory associations, shady images of low life, ghetto crime rings, the night-side of the world. But Bloom's cherubic, bespectacled face lent a certain absurd dignity to the idea of blowing my first joint. So I gave in. Kellner demonstrated how to inhale, then slowly exhale. Wilhelm cheered, snatching the joint from my fingers each time I toked.

5

At first I felt nothing. One, two, three, . . .the joints went round, round and round, and I puffed away, puffed dutifully, imitating my brethren. Still, nothing. I begin to wonder what all the fuss was about. I expected to become animated and loquacious like Bloom. I thought smoking marijuana was just looking and sounding like Bloom, philosophic clowning, a surreal game. I was entranced by Bloom, who sat on the floor and dominated us with an invincible torrent of amusing verbiage. Kellner and Wilhelm would break in now and then, and lamely give forth. But Bloom was king. Time passed, storms of words and laughter came and went, and on we went, and smoked and smoked, and then smoked some more.

My head, light as a fly, was swept away on winds of mad hilarity. I glanced across the cloud-filled room at a stack of books under an old lamp. My gaze stuck there for a moment; the books jumped at me. The worn red jacket of Hegel's *Phenomenology of Mind* glowed like a ruby. A heap of unlaundered shirts and socks sprang to life like a patch of primeval jungle. Bloom's filthy chaotic room was ablaze with mysterious beauty.

6

"Let's head for the West End," Kellner said. A cafe ten blocks north on Broadway. Wilhelm, sprawled on the floor, meditating on the ceiling bulb, grunted approval, and Bloom stopped talking. It was when Bloom shut up that the stillness screamed. A horn beeped, like a trumpet of doom. Was that a woman or a wild bird crying? I looked out the window at half-cleared skies. The rain had stopped and a lurid-looking moon peeked high over the Hudson River.

No question about it! I was beginning to feel different—*very* different. I stood up and stepped toward the window. My legs felt out of synch with the floor. What the hell, am I levitating? Am I about to become the flying philosopher? At first I felt pleasantly dizzy, then queasy. Riding down the antique elevator, I thought we'd never make it to the bottom. The light in the elevator was very bright.

Out in the street, the nightmare began.

No longer sitting in a circle in Bloom's apartment, the illusion of solidarity vanished. The four of us spread out and we began to head north on Broadway. The crowds of people, cars, storefronts, wet pavements smashed into my consciousness with shocking clearness. Extreme clearness created extreme strangeness. Everything looked so big! Bulgy, like growths pushing out of a fourth dimension.

Odd spatial drama. Way back down in a long forgotten room, something about Alice getting smaller and smaller.

I looked at a piss-stained bag of rotting garbage. A man plunged his hand inside, pulled out a crushed milk-container.

Up from Riverside a cold wind came slashing like a maniac, and rain started to fall again. Sharp raindrops stung my face. The coldness drove me back into my mind, away from my body, away from the solid world. Off in the distance, I hear my boots scraping along the cement pavement. Like a set from an alien landscape: beer cans, cigarette butts, dogeared newspapers panned under my feet. The background pointers of the here and now were fading. I forgot the sky. New York vanished.

My companions disappeared in the throng. Where was Bloom? Was that his raincoat trailing in the wind? A shadow among strolling giants on Broadway. No more laughter. Was that Bloom talking with Kellner? Who was that in the rusty-brown leather jacket? Everything had changed, the frolic was over. Suddenly I found myself alone, alone in new way.

The light turned green. A car whizzed by. Remotely, far off, I sensed danger. Automobiles. Hit. Smash. Bones. Hospital. Yeah, man. Check it out. Watch out! Green means wait. Or does it mean run? A plane thundered overhead, making my breastbone hum like a tuning-fork. A newspaper truck roared by, wheel-splattering-dirty-puddle. Huge drops of dark, guilt-stained rain-water. Dope. Dirty, back-street doper.

7

Stuck on the curbstone, afraid to cross. Forgot how to read the signals. Forgot how to use eyes, legs. Out of synch. Out of body. Whirling backward, down the well of childhood memories.

Lost in New York City.

I came by the Queensboro Bridge from Astoria, on the 59th Street Bus. I knew the way, Steinway street my mooring. I had the world arranged. Over the East River, traveled by bus, wandered into Central Park. Wandered by the lake in the park. Bus back, a dime, getting late. I know where to find the bus, 59th Street and Second Avenue. But where's 59th Street?

I need directions. I need a guide, a god. I'm only a kid, getting smaller and smaller. And people, so tall. Giants! A giant man with a fat leather briefcase. I tug at his jacket, I look up at the giant skyscrapers, above the shoulders of the giant man.

"Mister," I ask, "which way to 59th Street?" He looks down from heaven at me—like a man god—waves his mighty arm, and roars: "Son, you're on it!"

8

I crossed 104th Street. Picked up my pace, looking for Bloom, looking for the others. I noticed up ahead what looked like Bloom's raincoat, Kellner's leather jacket. I felt transparent, shrunken, exposed. Anybody could see through me. Anybody could see I was a degenerate dope-fiend.

"Hey, slow up, guys, slow up," I said. Nobody seemed to recognize me. Wilhelm, Kellner, Bloom, in a huddle now, talking and whispering, stopping, moving on. They're talking, Bloom, still the leader, still spewing words, words, words. I sidle up beside him, tap him on the shoulder. Doesn't see me, doesn't turn around.

"Kellner!" I say. Doesn't turn around.

"What's up, Wilhelm?" Same treatment.

"I didn't think it would be like this," I say, raising my voice. My voice surprises me. I think. I think of Descartes.

"That's a lot of joints for somebody who never smoked reefer. Why the hell doesn't somebody talk to me?"

Nobody hears me. "Back up in Bloom's we were all buddy-buddy, what happened?" I was shrinking, fading into non-being. "It's pretty weird," I said. I felt like the smile of the Cheshire cat.

I walked beside Bloom, but he didn't turn his head when I spoke. I slowed up, tried to get Wilhelm's attention. Blank on Wilhelm, too. I reached with rubbery fingers toward Kellner. His leather jacket was *too* soft, and my fingers seemed to pass through him. I tried to crunch my toes in my boots, but felt no sensations in my feet. I looked around. Broadway was silent. Soundless silhouettes, faces sphinx-like and remote.

What's happening? Am I really here? Am I dead?

Thinking this, I overheard Kellner say: "You seen Grosso?" Bloom answered solemnly: "No, I haven't. What about you?" Wilhelm shook his head. Bloom turned and looked right through me. "That's funny," he said. "I'll say," said Kellner, who shook *his* head, looking through me.

"Did we lose him somewhere?" asked Wilhelm, looking perplexed.

"You think he's anywhere anymore?" Bloom whispered.

"I'm right here," I said, loud enough for all three to hear. But nobody turned, and a new fear swept over me. Not like I expected, I kept thinking to myself. I thought I noticed a sardonic tone in Kellner's voice, a tone meant to say it was a joke—and that I really did exist. I clung to that tone, that raft. We continued walking, my three companions a few feet ahead of me.

Meanwhile, another part of my self was observing what was happening. Far back in the quiet depths of soul, a detached observer knows exactly what is happening. It flickers very softly in the shadows, very faintly.

I reasoned. No, they can't be kidding me. Maybe I'm not here, after all. Maybe I'm back in Bloom's hellhole, dreaming this. I flashed on Descartes again. Descartes sitting before his stove, meditating, noting to himself how he couldn't be certain whether or not he was dreaming. Descartes was right. There was nothing about the present scene, nothing in the quality of my sensations that said I wasn't dreaming. I was having a nightmare, that was it, that's why nobody saw me, nobody heard me. A case of lucid dreaming, a false awakening.

Again, Bloom: "I wish I knew where Grosso is. I'm starting to get a little worried." Kellner and Wilhelm nodded. We walked on, each block consuming an eternity of time. I know I'm in some kind of time warp. I stay close to my fellow philosophy students, yet feel myself dematerializing. I want to stop some stranger on the street and ask if he can see me, but can't bring myself to do it. Every now and then, as if in a recurring ritual, someone says: "Have you seen Grosso?" "Not me." "No, not for a while."

Reduced to ghost-status, I begged for the blood of attention, the blood of another consciousness to recognize, to revive, to resurrect me. Eviscerated, dismembered, disembowelled. The strong, vibrant me-stuff, drained, flushed out. All connecting fibers cut, legs walking machinelike on dead streets.

A creature of pure consciousness, I needed others to define me, to endow me with life. My soul, shorn from its habitual landmarks, adrift: centerless, like some spore floating through space, looking to land somewhere, to latch on to a tangible clod of earth.

9

At the West End Bloom turned and said: "Eat something." That was it. The joke was over. I ordered a hamburger. A moist leaf of lettuce brought me back to my senses. I discovered that this enhanced consciousness had other, humbler uses, like turning a second-rate hamburger into a repast of gods. I found my way back into cells, sinews, organs of sense perception. The inner scenes where I fought against the demons of nonbeing faded, and the laughter, now subdued, and the philosophic clowning, began all over again. I concluded that my companions had no idea how powerfully suggestive their little game had been.

10

It was a lesson to learn about the power of the imagination. I imagined myself right out of existence! I think, therefore I am nothing! I ejected myself into the outer reaches of oblivion, the land of no return, the Hades of my own soul. The drug magnified the process, helped me experience my self-induced flight to limbo with tremendous vividness. I felt the darkness close over me, the blood chill in my veins, the living core of my soul shrivel up. I felt myself thin to a gas of nonbeing. All self-inflicted.

The Demon within, the Inner Saboteur, the spirit that likes to diminish us. I made a discovery that night about this Demon: It was inside me, watchful, waiting to come out and do its mischief. Thanks to the drug, I had a chance to observe the Inner Saboteur under high magnification.

I was also alerted to the presence of a Hidden Observer, a calm lord of good will, an inner surveyor of everything. The whole drama was carefully noted, the absurdity underscored, the lesson learned.

But the Hidden Observer was not fully awake. Still, I did learn something. Never again would I blunder quite so ineptly into an ambush of my own contriving. Next time it would be harder to be tricked by the Inner Saboteur.

11

The story doesn't end here. Thanks to my introduction to the plant, I learned something else about soul. The aftereffect continued into the next day. What I felt is hard to describe in words. Of course, it would be easy to stick a label on it. I was "high." Psychologists might talk about pleasure-centers.

Say what you like; this is how it felt: The day after was cool and dry, a fine autumn day in New York. I went for a walk on Broadway after class, moving southeast across Central Park to the Frick Museum, then back on to Fifth Avenue. Walking—always something I loved for its own sake—was now raised to a new grade of pleasure. The effect of the infamous Killer Weed, lingering from the night before, produced in me a strange lucid pleasure that pervaded my consciousness.

The trees and birds of the park looked bright, and gave a curious pleasure. So did the strong feel of my legs bounding along and the tart air I breathed. Wherever I placed my attention, I detected the same elusive quality. Whatever I thought, or perceived, or imagined, seemed to glow with a nameless radiance. Talking with a musician in the park, playing with kids by the sailboats, pausing before the sea lions in the zoo: They all shimmered with the same rarefied understated delight.

Even dark scenes, riff-raff images, dogshit, rot, scum on the pavements, the prospect of time and its endless trail of wreckage, old gloomface, death—the works. A divine breeze of bliss wafted across the field of my consciousness. Whatever gray, bedraggled thing passed there became an occasion for a blessing.

Reflecting on this, it seems to me that I had that day a kind of experimental proof of Hindu metaphysics: namely, the idea of *sat-chit-ananda.* Now this Sanskrit expression always struck me as having a wonderful significance, an idea thoroughly bold and intriguing. It asserts that being (*sat*) is mind (*chit*), and that the intrinsic nature of all mind stuff is bliss, divine pleasure (*ananda*). In short, there is something about just being conscious—quite apart from *what* you're conscious of—that is intrinsically good, intrinsically blissful.

If one could detach one's consciousness from things, one might better learn to experience this blessedness, said to soak through the heart and soul of being. The great Eastern metaphysicians worked out methods for inducing states of mind that proved their metaphysics. Nor were they averse to using *bhang* — also known as the "poor man's paradise." Thanks to the nine joints Bloom laid on me that night, I caught a glimpse of *this* elusive dimension of the human soul.

12

Bit by bit, I was shoring up good news from my experiences, my experiments. My outlaw experiences revealed some startling messages from the Universe. It would be foolish not to listen. But I would have to piece the meaning together myself. It is a solitary path of exploration, the path each of us has to travel to discover the unknown God—the unknown depths of soul.

May I not fear the bands of peaceful and
wrathful deities—my own thought-forms.
The Tibetan Book of the Dead

Chapter Six

Christ and Satan: The Liquefaction of Opposites

Other psychic discoveries lay before me, thanks to those curious magnifying glasses—the psychedelics. An insight into the deeper operations of the soul I owe to Lola—an artist and friend of mine who lived on Third Avenue in New York's lower Manhattan.

2

Before we get into the steamy details, I want to say a few things about how these chemicals may act upon the brain. The intriguing question is: How could a poison expand human consciousness? It does seem a paradox. However, since the psychedelic Sixties, another, and parallel, paradox, has come to our attention. I mean the so-called Near-Death Experience.

The parallel is this: How could the most dangerous "toxin" of them all—being near death—result in the expansion of human consciousness? It is a paradox that nearly dying may, at least for some people, turn into the most extraordinary time of their life.

Researchers say there is a pattern to these remarkable experiences: People on the threshold of death often seem to glimpse new worlds, meet mysterious beings of light, and acquire dramatically new ideas about the nature of reality. No less remarkable, they are said to return with renewed spiritual values and increased psychic powers.

Is there a connection between the two paradoxes? I think there may be, but to clarify it we have to say something about how brain and consciousness relate—an ancient riddle of philosophy.

Materialism states that consciousness is identical with, or, at any rate, a by-product of, what goes on in the brain. The consequences are clear. As you diminish or destroy brain function, you automatically diminish or destroy consciousness. The verdict on immortality: Death of brain implies death of consciousness.

But this is only one among possible models for the relation between brain and consciousness. According to such luminaries as Plato, Bishop Butler, F.S. Schiller, William James, C. D. Broad, and Henri Bergson, the brain, rather than produce, is said to detect, transmit, or filter consciousness. A crude analogy with radio and radio waves: The radio does not produce the radio waves; it detects, transmits, and filters them. If your radio breaks down, it doesn't follow that the sounds you're listening to have ceased to exist. They just cease to be detectable. An analogy is possible between this and the mind-brain relationship.

Aldous Huxley tried to explain why mescaline or LSD expand our consciousness. According to Huxley, when you ingest one of these sacred poisons, you block the brain from performing its function as filter of consciousness. You lose psychophysical coordination—are less efficient in the everyday business of life. But you are compensated with an expansion of consciousness. The brain, on this theory, works like a filter for Mind at Large. Screw up the filter with a drug, and you open the floodgates to Mind at Large.

Two other areas of research support Huxley's theory. I've already mentioned the first: research showing that the ultimate toxic experience, nearly dying, may sometimes expand consciousness. Support also comes from parapsychology. Research shows that psychic function increases when the brain idles and attention is shifted from external events to internal states. Meditation, dreaming, and hypnosis, for example, produce effects similar to those of psychedelics: They cause the brain to idle, impede its filtering function, thus opening inlets in us to the mothersea of Mind at Large.

3

As I log the sea changes of my world-picture, I note experiences showing the living nature of symbols and archetypes that rise up from this mothersea. (By "archetype" I mean a universal image with power to fascinate and dominate consciousness.) So powerful have these experiences been that I sometimes feel the need to resist and observe them, keeping at bay their seductive magic.

I want to describe how one of these archetypes came to life, so to speak, right before my eyes. Since it was projected on me from another person, I was able to observe its effects with detachment. The power of these ancient images is great. As powers on the loose in our internal environment, they demand our respect and invite our effort to understand them. Sometimes they temporarily possess us, and when that happens, heaven can pour out its secrets or hell unleash its demons.

4

Lola may have looked delicate, but she was strong enough to build her own canvas stretchers and tough enough to handle the drunks on Third Avenue. One of her teeth had been chipped from a motorbike accident, an imperfection lost in her sweet smile. Lola was a gentle soul, and always saw the bright and agreeable side of things. She did the unexpected, like give a man a bouquet of flowers. Happiness for her was having a little extra cash to buy exotic lotions from Khiel's old apothecary, down the block on 13th Street.

A poor art teacher at the local high school, she made her simple furnishings look rich: a colorful stone here, a silken fabric there. Her watercolors, given to conjuring a single pale violet mood, decked her apartment walls. A fine artist, Lola's greatest art was her self—the way she lived, the way she made you feel in her presence: welcome—right to the core of your being.

5

So it was hard to say no, one November afternoon, when she offered me a hit of Clear Light. Clear Light? That was the name of a particular brand of LSD. Lola was friends with a dealer from the West Coast, a former political science professor from the City University of New York. Roger, like many liberals of the period, was convinced the country was going through a grave crisis. He went to anti-war rallies, wrote letters to congressmen, lent a hand to draft-dodgers. But he came to feel that by distributing Clear Light, a potent changer of human consciousness, he was doing the best thing he could for the country. Roger loved to read from the works of William Godwin, the anarchist philosopher, as he doled out the tiny squares of LSD to friends and customers.

I should say something about the choice of name—Clear Light—which I think was lifted from the *Tibetan Book of the Dead.* That profound treatise of Eastern psychology was a lifelong companion of C. G. Jung's. Many viewed it as useful for mapping the stages of the psychedelic journey. Clear Light was a perfect name for LSD. Its great virtue was to cast a brilliant beam of clear light on consciousness, opening a clearing into the hells and heavens of the unconscious.

6

Lola and I dropped the acid and ended up in bed. (The amount I took was small, the effect on me slight.) Not so Lola. I was about to observe a remarkable display of projection, a display confirming the teachings of the Tibetan Book of the Dead, in which the dark and light side of the divine is alternately projected upon the same neutral canvas. As it turned out, the neutral canvas was going to be me! It was a tricky situation, not without danger. But in the end, we hit upon a stunning solution.

7

After making love, I noticed Lola staring at me. A look of horror had come over her.

"Lola!" I said. "Was it that bad?"

She kept on staring, her eyelids arched with disbelief. Her staring was so intense, it made my hair stand up. Lola looked transfigured. Something had taken hold of her. She made a sudden move to slide from my casual embrace.

I held her, and said: "Lola, what's wrong?"

Her large blue eyes, moist with tears, were fixed on my beard. She began to sob. Her hand, trembling, reached for the gold cross hanging from her neck.

Then she said, her voice hoarse with deep emotion: "You're the devil, aren't you?"

"Beg your pardon," I said.

"You're Satan! Tell me the truth!" she said, raising her voice.

I was nonplussed, and started to laugh. Again she said: "Why didn't you tell me you were Satan?"

I was flattered, of course. But really—Satan? I admit my face was more lean than round, and I had a beard that lengthened my chin, but befitting a bookish man, not enough to warrant comparison with Mephistopheles. When I laughed—it was just a good-natured giggle—it drove poor Lola into even greater depths of despair.

"You see, you see!" she cried, "You laugh just like the devil." Saying this, she jumped out of bed, naked but for one red stocking dangling from her foot, and ran to the door.

"I'm going downstairs, I'm going to *tell* everybody!"

I was about to lunge to stop her. The apartment was on the ground floor. It had turned cold—it was early winter—and big snowflakes were falling.

Lola stood by the door, whimpering. Something told me not to budge.

"It's snowing, Lola," I said, trying to sound calm. I pointed to the window, down toward the street, where slush was piling up. Her hand gripped the doorknob—that strong wiry hand that looked so deceptively delicate. I watched the veins and taut sinews. She looked ready to charge out the door onto Third Avenue.

All of a sudden, her look changed. An invisible force wiped the creases from her brow. The look of horror changed to a look of rapture.

"No," she cried, "you're not Satan. You're Christ!"

Now she was transported with loving bliss.

"Oh, sweet Jesus!" she cried with feeling, and rushed across the room, embracing me. Lola was petite, but she tossed me on the bed, as if I were a rubber doll. She leaped on top of me, and gazed blissfully into my eyes. She moaned that I was Jesus Christ.

Well, I thought, this is an improvement. "Look, Lola," I said, "I'm just me. Remember? Your friend. We were having fun, just being ourselves."

"No," she said, outraged, "you *are* Christ!"

She had the splayed look of Bernini's Saint Teresa. Not a hint of doubt in her voice. An alien rapt gaze was all I could discern.

Determined to convince her I was made of mortal flesh, I wrapped my hands round her thighs, and pressed her toward me with unabashed human ardor. I hoped this would knock her out of her Christ projection.

"Hey, baby," I said, stroking her, trying like mad to sound as un-Christlike as possible. When I said this, she changed her expression again and switched back into seeing me as Satan.

"I'm going downstairs," she wailed, "I'm going to report you to the police."

So the cycle began all over again. I noticed a pattern. When she backed away and looked at me from a distance, something clicked and she saw me in my benign aspect. When she drew close and responded sexually, she would turn on me and howl that I was from the dark side. I tried to reason with her, but all the logic in the world was useless against the psychic forces the drug had unleashed.

The Christ-Satan archetype was alive and well in that room with us. I had become a walking movie screen, upon which Lola, through the "Clear Light" of her imagination, was projecting the awesome psychodrama of salvation and damnation. I had known her two years and never spotted any sign of craziness; but there she was, raving like a madwoman, saying in one breath I was her God, and in the next that I was the leading fallen angel himself. My biggest fear was that she'd get violent, and run out into the street.

I tried to explain to her the psychology of the Tibetan Book of the Dead. If she was in the Satan mode, my talking made me more satanic in her eyes. If she was in the Christ mode, what I said didn't matter—she was beyond reason. I was worn out, especially from her jumping on me in the Christ mode.

8

At wit's end, I had to figure a way to convince Lola I was neither Jesus Christ nor Satan. Nothing I said or did seemed to make any difference. I had become a piece of furniture in her dream world. Something had to happen to deflate her wild projections.

Lola was resting with comparative ease on top of me—she was in the Christ mode. Her long sandy curls brushed my eyes. Although the apartment was well-heated, her hands felt cold. I recalled my first psychedelic adventure. It was the taste of lettuce that enabled me to return to concrete reality; after a few bites of a hamburger, I got a hold on myself. I glanced around the room. Nothing to eat—just a bottle of wine.

"Lola," I said, pointing toward the bottle. "Care for a sip of wine?"

She squatted on me, her glazed eyes peering in the distance, peering right through me, it seemed, into realms of Mind at Large—beyond booze. I feared doing anything that would set her off into the perilous fantasy that I was the Dark One. I glanced meekly into her wide bright eyes, trying to appear as humdrum as possible, like a man scanning a telephone directory.

At that moment she looked down on me. Gone was the look of otherworldly rapture, and in its place was a more earthy glimmer. Her lips quivered—nearly a normal smile. Her body was still tense but she gave out with a soft groan, a more easygoing, Lola-like groan.

"What is it?" I asked.

"I have to pee," she said.

"Well," I said, starting to move away, delighted with the news. If something so humble could distract her even for a moment from her craziness, I'd be grateful. Without moving, she held me fast beneath her, and repeated: "I have to pee."

Again I said I was glad to hear of this and started to yank my thigh from under her. But she held me down, and said with shocking finality: "I want to do it *on you.*" I was startled by what seemed like an uncharacteristic request of Lola's. Lola had been to Catholic school, and I understood her head being full of Christ and the Devil. But this?

Yet there she was, big fierce mad blue eyes staring, and waiting. She was waiting for a reply. She was waiting for permission to urinate on me. The alternative was another round of the Christ-Satan routine. I was bruised and nerve-racked. I thought of the good effect eating had on me—when I was once stuck in a weird psychic bardo. Maybe, I guessed, this will help.

"Go ahead," I said, gallantly.

The effect was somehow instantly to bring Lola back down to earth. The spell was broken, and the archetypes of Christ and Satan melted—like snowflakes hitting the warm gutters of Third Avenue.

*Welcome, O life! I go to encounter for the
millionth time the reality of experience and to
forge in the smithy of my soul theuncreated
conscience of my race.*

James Joyce
Portrait of the Artist as a Young Man

PART FOUR
Sacred Symbols
and the Soul

Born Catholic, I inherited a neat idea of my soul and its
destiny. The rules for the journey of life were written down in
my Baltimore catechism. None of it quite worked for me.

Since we inhabit an evolving universe, I like to think of
myself as an evolutionary catholic—accent on lower case "c."
Kata holon—catholic—this good Greek word means "universal." I believe we are all evolutionary catholics today, that is,
whether we realize it or not, we're all being forced to work
through our native symbols and archetypes toward a new, a
universal myth of meaning. Without a universal myth of
meaning, how is our unruly species going to make it into the
Third Millennium? Here is something we all have in common:
the struggle to make new meaning. Whether we like it or not,
we're all soulmakers in an age of transformation. This is what
brings us together: the imperative to make, to create and
re-create ourselves—as James Joyce put it, to create for the
millionth time the "conscience of (our) race." The alternative
is to drift with the mass, to join the march of the soulless. In
the next two chapters I describe experiences that show how
"I"—that multiple, shifting focus I call myself—am still
entangled in my ancestral roots. There are bonds we feel with
the past that we don't understand or consciously assent to. In
Chapter 7, I report a curious haunting: the ancient Romans
spoke of *genii loci*—spirits of locale. These spirits, the ancient
Italians believed, haunt certain places—groves, grottos, hills.

So I found out in my visit to the Gargano, a mountain region in Southern Italy; the locale of my ancestors, it is a place of archangel visitations and other strange phenomena. In this angel- and madonna-haunted region, Padre Pio, a virtualextraterrestrial among us, a walk-in from God knows where, was reared. In this chapter, I tell of my close encounter with this remarkable man. Chapter 8 deals with the psychokinetic power of soul. Do we possess such power? In the incident described, it appears that something akin to soul power was responsible for the puzzling and synchronous flowering of a plant. This piece of animistic magic took place on Christmas Eve—a holiday, a holy day—a healing day. If there's a memorandum here for students of soulmaking, it is that something we used to call Sacred Time still has the power to create life from death.

We are explorers, ready for new departures.

Giorgio de Chirico

Chapter Seven
Close Encounter With Padre Pio

March, 1965; on my way to Amsterdam on a Norwegian freighter, the Black Tern. I got sick at sea—killer headaches from aspirin poisoning—but made it from Amsterdam to Paris, where I wandered around a while, then boarded the Orient Express, going south.

Three days and nights en route to Athens, I sat on a straight-back wooden seat, unable to sleep or move. A Greek, who said he had a metal bar in his head, fed me. By noon on the third day, I was in Athens. A few weeks of island hopping, and I was back to my old self. Restless for new landscapes, I bought a ticket at Piraeus for a boat to Italy.

I was about to experience—for want of a better word—a kind of haunting.

2

Italy! Land of my ancestors. Many a time back in New York I dreamt of this moment. I dreamt of visiting this enchanted country I knew only from books and from stories my father told me.

I stepped off the boat ramp and put my feet on real Italian soil. An odd vibration passed through me. For a while I walked in a daze, unsure of what I was feeling.

The haunting had begun.

I took out my map, got my bearings, and set out from the port of Brindisi to hitchhike up the Adriatic coast. It was a luminous April morning. The sun looked vaguely alive, like an eye tailing my movements. The color of the sky, a blue I couldn't place—of eyes I'd once seen somewhere between New York and Elfland.

Italy felt different. I had crossed into a different psychic zone. There was an influence here, an atmosphere congested with invisible presences.

The air smelled indolent. Walking along the road, a fruit truck stopped to give me a lift. A huge beefy hand held out a bunch of golden grapes. The man's voice was hoarse, abrupt, friendly. A few minutes later, he dumped me back on the road.

I glanced at the sky. At my right, an olive grove plunged toward the sea. I walked, and each step, each breath I took, it seemed I got giddier, drunker. My knapsack, stuffed with books, felt light as a feather. I stepped up my pace, feeling more buoyant. The rides I hitched were short, a few kilometers at a time. In between rides, I walked, tirelessly, all morning. I had no clear idea where I was going.

At Monopoli, the road veered toward the shore, and the sea came into view, along with rows of broken stone houses. The small waves splashed, splattered, and sent up a soft lazy foam. A curious languor stained the foam-flecked air. Unlike the turquoise Aegean, the Adriatic blue looked tattered, like an antique arras.

A driver, wearing white gloves, nodded for me to hop in. Elegant, lean-faced, cold-eyed. He liked to take the wild turn on the winding road. Kept asking if I was afraid. No, I said, lying. Next, a lingerie salesman gave me a lift; he wanted to know if I read Marcuse. Sure, I said, and we gabbed in broken Italian about Eros and the demise of lady's underwear.

3

The Marcuse man left me near the Church of San Nicola in the old part of Bari. I glanced up and down the desolate strada—a long lull in the traffic. An old man, sitting in the shade, nodded.

"Nothing will come now," he said, "Rest."

Bari is a busy seaport. Since ancient times, a way to the Levant. My mother's people came from Bari. Stories my mother told me—strange stories—came back as I walked the medieval cobblestone lanes. Stories retold over passing years, at odds with my world picture. My mother's tales, quaint—but somehow, a little less quaint, here in old Bari. Words and images, debris of childhood memories, washed up for inspection.

The man in the shade smiled, pointing a brown finger toward the cafe. He looked like mother's father, dead since my childhood. He had died on a hot humid day, she told me many times. Sitting by a window on East 12 Street, watching the kids playing in the street, a cold wind passed through her—a wind from nowhere. She looked at the clock: three in the afternoon. Later she found out; her father died at three o'clock.

Stories my mother told me.

Three months later she heard him breathing beside her. Her dead father murmuring in bedroom shadows. She knew the way her father breathed. A sick old man, he sat in the same chair, never spoke. She knew his moan.

"Papa!" she cried out. He was like a wind—like the wind that passed through her the summer day he died.

Stories. I always doubted them. I walked across the road to a small cafe, bought some lemonade, sat down at a wooden table. A skinny boy played on the rocks, tossing stones. I watched waves break against purple lichen, foam shatter in slow motion against a cloudless sky. Dulled by heat, entranced by surf, the stories came back.

My mother was pregnant with my sister, Anne. April 16, 1942, *five in the morning.* The votive candle flame suddenly shoots to the ceiling, filling the room with light. A flare from the beyond: It wakes her and she calls out.

"Go back to sleep," my father says.

"Something's wrong," she says. In the morning, bad news. Brother-in-law, East Side Highway, death crash—*five-in-the-morning.* My mother's thought world. Natural, here, it seemed, along this old coastal road; unnatural, in New York City. Stories. About the statue of St. Joseph on her vanity that kept turning its back on her before her mother died. St. Joseph, the patron saint of death. Sure. Fantastic. But then, mother didn't lie.

I got up and walked toward San Nichola's Basilica.

Inside, the air was cool and damp. I went down a winding stone stairway into the crypt below, my footsteps echoing on the high walls. To the right, three long candles were burning. A tremor in the air made the flames shudder. A voice was chanting in Latin. A sad "Dominus" rang through the darkly-lit catacomb.

I noticed a painting by an anonymous old master. Figure of Christ, emaciated, robed in lenten purple. Oh, yes, it was April—it was Lent. Outmoded ceremonies, of course. Or were they? What made me so sure? Perhaps these old stones and images held records of mysteries stranger than I could imagine. The painting grabbed my attention. The pigment looked bruised from the passage of time. There was something about the image, as if it were watching me—as if I heard a soft cry.

Pain murmured under painted thorns. A voice was calling. A lonely human voice calling people from the gay sunlight, calling bathers from the sea—calling hitchhikers from the road!

4

I went north again, past Bari, the road turning inland. The next big city was Foggia. The name of Foggia rang a bell. My mother use to talk of a Franciscan monk who lived near Foggia. He lived in a small mountain town called San Giovanni Rotondo. His name was Padre Pio.

Stories she told about him were strange.

A man of miracles, he bore the stigmata—those curious copies of the wounds of Christ. In his palms and feet, perfect circular holes, the size of a nickel. A long gash in his side. Mime of Christ—he bled for fifty years. And the blood, she had said, smelled of flowers.

Mother had *very* strange stories to tell of him. Bilocations, battles with demons, visions and transports. An old admirer of Saint Francis, that mystic freedom fighter, I listened to these stories, curious, intrigued, but also repelled. The dream I had before I sailed from New York, the great dream of the two Christs, came back. The eerie painting in the crypt of San Nicola brought it to mind. Christ of eternal struggle—false TV Christ.

Stories went through my head. I tried to brush them away. After all—I was on vacation! And I was reading *Being and Nothingness* not *The Imitation of Christ.* But stories of Padre Pio kept buzzing around inside me after stopping at San Nicola's crypt. Maybe it was the painting in the blue shadow, the mute cry of pain.

I thought about the Padre. This was a real live man, not a legend or item of history. I asked myself if I wanted to visit a monk said to have stopped American bombers during the Second World War by appearing in the sky and waving them back. Or a man who caused an eye—blown out of a worker's head from a dynamite accident—to re-materialize? Or a man who read your mind and knew every sin you ever committed? (That didn't thrill me.) Did I want to stand face to face with a monk often found on his cell floor in the morning, bruised from battling with demons all night?

5

Flanked by rows of gnarled olive trees and red stucco farm huts, I watched the dusty road shoot by. Riding to Foggia, I remembered a dream I had before sailing for Europe. *A cowled monk is writing words on a sandy path. I stoop down to see what he's writing. The monk whirls his brown skirt over the words and three white birds fly out of the ground.*

My sister was traveling in Europe. She got sick and stopped writing home. My father worried. There was a book about Padre Pio in the house with his picture on the cover. My father, not suggestible and none too religious, noticed something about the picture. A funny flutter. He looked down. In place of the Padre's face, as if through a little oval television screen, his daughter's face appears, flashing on and off.

This strange man, I thought to myself, isn't far from here. "*Dov' e Foggia?*" I asked the driver. He raised his head: "*Avanti, avanti . . . .*"

I knew that San Giovanni Rotondo was somewhere in the mountains of the Gargano, the spot on the map that looks like the spur of the Italian boot. Obscure feelings welled up inside me. Padre Pio came from Pietrelcina and spoke the same dialect as my father. My father emigrated from the Campania, the land around Naples, under the shadow of Vesuvius, facing the Tyrrhenian Sea. Both men came from the same rocky hills, the same solar landscapes. The further inland toward the Campania we drove, the more I felt drawn to the Gargano.

6

Padre Pio—what an ally to stretch one's idea of soul! To break the spell of that claustrophobic worldview I retained from my formal education. I found myself being led—apart from my conscious intention—to visit this place, so unlike the famous cities of Italy. Here was a place that bore a man whose life makes a joke of the metaphysics of modern science.

7

Genii loci—spirits that haunted places. Perhaps I was feeling the ghostly presences of the land, a kind of haunting of place. There were many odd things about the whole land belt from the Gargano to Naples. Many prodigies are reported of the region. There was, for instance, the mystery of the ebullition of blood in the Naples Cathedral: The dried blood of an old Roman martyr, sealed in a reliquary, liquefies during annual ceremonies, in full view of cheering celebrants. There were other flesh and blood prodigies, like the stone of Pozzuoli that bleeds and the Eucharist wafer of Lanciano that turned into flesh.

People of volcanic imagination. The ley of Vesuvius, steeped in antique legends. Some tall tales of angels. The town of Monte Sant' Angelo is devoted to the cult of St. Michael, the great warrior archangel and defender of the faith. The highest peak of the Gargano peninsula is Monte Sant' Angelo, circled by arid slopes, dotted with gorse and white stones. The shepherds still wear their ancestor's rough garb.

In 490 A.D. pagans ruled the Gargano. One day, the story goes, the lord of the hill was about to sacrifice a bull at the mouth of a cavern. The bull wobbled, as if entranced. The pagan lord shot at the bull but the arrow turned around and pierced him. Saint Michael appeared, declared a moratorium on bull killing, and proclaimed the cave sacred to himself.

The budding Christian community was besieged by savage hordes of Odoacre. However, Michael the Archangel came to the rescue, and rained sand and hail on the barbarians. The Prince of the Heavenly Host appeared once again to consecrate the cavern. In 1656 when plague ravaged the Gargano, he appeared and instructed the people to bless stones from the grotto; the stones became power objects and were used for healing. The tower of Saint Michael's basilica testifies to this ancient cult.

8

Padre Pio, miracle worker, grew up where miracles were matters of common sense. A man confessed he didn't believe in God. Pio looked at him: "You're crazy!"

Southern Italy venerates the Virgin Mary. The Goddess has always claimed this place where blood prodigies proliferate. In Pietrelcina, the Padre's birthplace, the cult of Mary flourished —the cult of Our Lady of Pompeii.

A story of the Padre's childhood is worth remembering. Little Franco and his dad, Mr. Forgione, didn't have VCRs or computer games to amuse them on holidays. They went instead to the shrine of Our Lady of Pompeii. Once, when Franco was five, they tuned in to a strange show. They came upon a crowd watching a woman begging Our Lady for help. The woman was holding a misshapen hydrocephalic child; she screamed at the statue of Mary: "You won't cure him! Then take him!" she said, dashing the child against the stone altar.

It looked like death for the boy but he just stood up, and walked away, healed. Not a bad substitute for a music video. Till life's end, Padre Pio prayed to Our Lady of Pompeii.

9

I reached Foggia by late afternoon, still meaning to go as far north as possible. But I was fated to visit San Giovanni Rotondo, the famed monastery where Padre Pio had lived for half a century. The image of the bearded Capuchin haunted me. I admired a man so devoted to serving humanity. And I was fascinated by a man who daily defied the religion of ordinary reality. The more I thought of the Padre, the more I felt a certain animation, an unaccountable rise in spirits. Perhaps, I thought in earnest, I should visit Padre Pio.

10

But the attraction met the counter-force of reflection. For one thing, I wanted to disentangle this quality—this promise of super-normal joy—from the creed that inspired and gave it form. The creed was magnificent, like a ruined cathedral, a monument to visit and cherish; but after traveling in the mental country of Walt Whitman, that great soul of the open road, I was wary of creeds. Yet despite my misgivings, a force kept tugging me toward the Padre's mountain retreat.

11

I asked a policeman for directions to San Giovanni Rotondo. Vaguely he pointed: "*Avanti, avanti.*" I walked to the edge of town. The road stretched in the distance, lined with cypress trees slanting steeply toward the horizon, the wind blowing from the setting sun. The further I walked, the more the road became desolate. Shadows lengthened and the air of twilight chilled.

A small deserted factory whose roof had collapsed appeared on my right. A man stepped out from behind a broken door, waving a large white handkerchief. He looked distracted, and walked halt-ingly. Perhaps he lived nearby. He seemed to be out for a stroll. The fields were empty as far as I could see. Nothing but the abandoned factory, cypress converging on the horizon, the apex of the road's long triangle.

"San Giovanni Rotondo?"

He didn't hear me. I waved my hand. Eyelids down, he seemed calm, at home in the middle of nowhere. Wearing a light brown overcoat, a little stooped, older than I first thought, he walked as if each step cost him a small pain. Yet he looked composed, strolling pensively through the grasses, through shadows of late afternoon. Again, I asked: "San Giovanni?" His voice trailed, "Si, si, si . . . ."

A car appeared. A young man with pink cheeks and bright brown eyes braked. A few kilometers, left me off, pointing to a side road into the hills. A sole hawk glided above us. Another driver stopped and gave me a lift. The closer I came to the monastery, the easier the rides came. It seemed odd, being far from the main road.

12

Upon arrival I found my way to Mary Pyle, an American devotee who ran a small boarding house for pilgrims. The room was small, wooden floors and walls bare but for a crucifix above the bed. Padre Pio's parents stayed in this house. The window overlooked a stark landscape of small hills. Mary Pyle, heavyset, wearing a plain dress, walked slowly. A native New Yorker of good family and education, she was unwell. She spoke gently.

"You can go to mass tomorrow," she said, "five in the morning. You better get up early and be there in plenty of time. It gets very crowded, and you'll want a seat."

The Padre's Masses were legendary. They brought you back to the Crucifixion, people said. His wounds bled abnormally during the rite. Devotees cherish the bloodstained undergarments as holy relics.

"There's something else," she said very softly. "If you want to speak to Padre Pio, you can; you can become one of his spiritual sons."

Her remark took me by surprise. I nodded politely, but the idea was daunting. It was enough for the moment to think about going to Mass, a practice I had given up long ago. This would be different, everyone said. The town women fought like alley cats to be near him in church; some of them spread nasty rumors about Pio, providing ammunition for his detractors.

13

After dinner, I walked up the hill to my room. It was getting darker, and deep blue dyed the evening sky. The wind was blowing, the window creaked and rattled, sparrows twittered on the eaves. I turned the lamp on. A dim yellowish bulb, typical in old Italian homes. Tired from the long day, I drifted to the edge of sleep. Images of my first impressions of Italy came back: the haunted sea, like a blue waking dream; the broken stone houses; the dry thoughtful landscape. The cypress on the road from Foggia rose before my mind's eye, sloping toward the dying sunset. The man in the vacant fields came back. And the painted Christ, calling to passers-by on the road through old Bari.

I heard a scratching at my door. Light, high-pitched laughter. Two thin ladies—pilgrims from Sicily—wanted to have a word with me. One spoke rapidly of miracles; most of her teeth were missing. The other's eyes sparkled, laughing when I tried to speak. They patted me affectionately. Bewildering creatures! What an eerie glow of happiness they seemed to have! They warned me about getting up early. You had to be first on line, if you wanted a good seat. This was the sacred rite. Man and God were going to commune. The Padre knew how to do it.

"Goodnight, ladies."

After reading a while, I turned off the lamp and tried to sleep. An old house high on a windy hill, the trees seemed to whisper in tongues. Tossing and turning, I felt like a guilty child who had strayed from his father's garden.

I was one of them, I thought. And yet I wasn't, I answered. Back and forth, I argued with myself. In the room, pacing back and forth, phantoms of an ancient brotherhood.

I fell asleep.

Sitting in an empty church, I hear footsteps. A courier, wearing a brilliant blue shirt, ragged shimmering silk. "Your father is sick." I look up at the altar. A great wooden crucifix has toppled down, blocking the central aisle.

I turned on the light, and looked at my watch. Nearly five. I looked out the window. Near dawn, the wind had died down, and birds were chirping away. What did it mean? My father sick? Which father? My father back home in New York, Father Pio, the Heavenly Father? Was God calling me? Or was it just a trick of the unconscious? A goad to drive me back into the fold, the ancient brotherhood?

What about Sartre? Darwin? Einstein? What about Shankara? Chuang Tzu? Black Elk? I lay in bed and wondered. It made me uncomfortable, all these presences, dreams, tribal memories. How did it all come together? Was life just a crazy quilt chaos we had to rip a piece from? Make it all hang together, a pleasing circle or a stark cross or a soaring thunderbird? I leaned back in bed, and fell into sleep. When I awoke, I knew I had missed Mass.

14

I walked around town after coffee. Later, I found Mary Pyle, and told her my plans to leave.

"Don't go yet," she said. "You can still see Padre Pio. He's giving benediction today."

"What time?" I ask impatiently.

"Around two."

Toward two I went into the new church of Saint Mary's. A small crowd was gathering at the doorway. My two Sicilian friends were there, sporting to bathe in the supernatural afflux. I stood apart from the crowd, waiting under the balcony.

Then Padre Pio appeared, the Capuchin brothers supporting him by his elbows as he shuffled into view.

I looked up, glimpsing the dark fingerless mittens which he wore to conceal his wounds. They were covered with unsightly crusts that fell off his hands at intervals. Though I didn't know it at the time, he was ill. He was also being persecuted—by people within the Church.

He chanted the benediction, a distant hoarse drone, tired and resigned—a voice sounding from another world. He paused and raised his hands, blessing us below. I moved with the crowd, as it moved toward the right. The Padre stopped, stooped a little, groaned. The brothers bore with him, standing close, standing behind him. He moved again, shuffling toward the right side of the balcony. The crowd lurched after him, murmuring prayers, shouting pleas. He made the sign of the cross, blessed us again, and started to walk off the arched terrace.

Suddenly he stopped. Slowly, very slowly, as if he was pondering something, he started to turn. I was standing by myself, off to the side. He turned toward me, stopping halfway, hesitating. Then slowly again, as if he were still pondering, he turned back and disappeared from the terrace.

15

How fleeting and yet how much that last gesture has stuck in my mind! As though he mimicked my half-completed move toward him, meeting me only half-way. Maybe he decided to leave me alone, respecting my need to travel my own path—my need to explore on my own. Or maybe it was not as I thought, and there was no contact, no meaningful half-gesture.

16

So many strange tales. They say he controlled the weather and commanded the behavior of animals. A lady couldn't wake up on time for mass. Well, according to an American monk I met there, Father Joseph Pious Martin, the Padre sent a bird to wake her every morning. The bird became her alarm clock. But he did more for the sleepy signorina. A troop of dogs picked her up at her doorstep every morning and escorted her to church.

After benediction, I strapped my knapsack to my back, walked to the edge of town, and stuck out my thumb, *per fare l'autostop*. No problem getting a ride into the Gargano, I figured a ride out would be just as easy. I was wrong; nobody stopped for me. After a while, I saw I wasn't going to catch a ride.

I waved at a passing car. I might have been invisible—not even a nod. Funny, I thought. Unheard of in Italy! I went looking for the bus to Foggia. I recalled the stories about the Padre's reputed ability to control rain, to make birds and dogs do his bidding. What folly! How could anyone believe such things? Yet here I was, waiting for a bus. Did the Padre arrange it so nobody would give me a lift out of town?

17

The clock on the train station's slate-green wall had stopped. Slumped on the bench, I watched lizards dart across the sun-scorched tracks. Afternoon threw an orange pallor on the gray platform. Departure in half an hour. I dozed. Footsteps startled me. A child on the far side of the tracks was running from the ticket counter. A woman with long dark hair called after him. She grabbed the child's hand, scolding him, but he shook himself free, and bolted. He was playing with a rubber tire, babbling excitedly to himself. The boy glanced at his mother, as he rolled the tire to the end of the platform. I looked up and down the tracks, then at the slate-green wall. A shadow now shrouded the clock's face.

We know and can know very little about the New Nature. The task of the imagination here is not to forecast it but simply, by brooding on many possibilities, to make room for a more complete and circumspect agnosticism.
C. S. Lewis
Miracles

Chapter Eight

A Christmas Card From Heaven

I was living in Edgewater, New Jersey, in a small brick house overlooking the Hudson river. It was Christmas Eve, and bitter cold. It was the coldest night of the year. It had fallen to zero, and it was windy as hell.

2

The roads were covered with ice; driving Francesca home would be risky. People could barely walk straight, it was so windy. Through the large front window I watched a few brave souls, struggling past us up the hill. Good to be indoors! Away from crowds—the usual Christmas fanfare. I was content to spend Christmas Eve alone with Francesca. But Francesca wanted to go to Midnight Mass.

I had to respect her wish, but the truth is I wasn't inclined to attend church. I offered to go to Mass in the morning, when things warmed up a little. I reminded her how much she disliked the cold, but she insisted on Midnight Mass. Francesca had a temper like a quantum cat sitting on a hot tin roof, and I preferred to avoid trouble.

3

Francesca was also an intriguing person. For one thing, she claimed to see fairies. Tiny creatures with delicate phosphorescent wings, now and then, glided past her—mostly, I should add, when she was a child. It happened when she was alone, playing in her backyard or tossing sleeplessly in bed. She told me of these sightings many times, and I believe she was describing a real experience. They made a popping sound, she said, a high-pitched whistle. She said she heard tiny screams— beings who desperately wanted to be heard.

She remembered the sounds her fairies made long after she stopped seeing them; and they became her inspiration to study flute and piccolo. She practiced many hours every day, hours most kids spent outdoors having fun. Francesca was different. She wanted to recapture the whistling sound of her childhood companions.

Her parents laughed at her tales of fairy music. Francesca's friends thought she was on drugs. Strange as her stories were, I listened, as I always do to stories from the far side—with interest and respect.

I also admired Francesca's doggedness. She started out with a poor ear for music, but kept on practicing, gradually improving, till one day it became apparent to all that will had triumphed over nature. Thanks to the inspiration of her fairy companions, Francesca became a fine flutist.

4

Still, I had to worry about her temper. Her outbursts could be so unexpected, the thought of them was a mild but constant threat to my peace of mind. I was more her weatherman than her lover: forever trying to predict—but usually being taken off guard by— the next thunderbolt or flash flood.

That night I felt pretty secure. After all, I could rely upon her Christmas spirit. What could go wrong?

5

I pointed to the green and amber lights of the Manhattan skyline, shimmering on the ice floes. But Francesca was relentless about church and in the end bullied me into going.

I put on my coat, and out we went. Icy gusts of wind at once slapped us in the face. Up the hill we dragged ourselves, our teeth chattering all the way. The church was located by the public library in Fort Lee. At the corner of Main and Palisade, we were greeted by an American Flag, a Christmas Tree, and the Jewish Menorah. It was near midnight when we passed Green's Funeral Parlor, for some sinister reason festively ablaze with lights.

"Let's stand in the back," I whispered.

All the seats were taken. They were out in force, the Christmas Eve Christians, the Midnight Mass Crashers. I had never been inside before; it was a drab, cold-looking modern church. I was struck by the bustle and movement, the sort you find in shopping malls. In fact, that was how I felt: as though we were in a shopping mall. It felt like a big sale was going on. The sale was causing a certain amount of excitement. Heads bobbed about impatiently, eyes peered across the church, fur coats rustled against the pews. Restless youngsters streamed in, sniffling with cherry-red noses, all jammed together under the stations of the Cross.

I leaned over and murmured into Francesca's ear: "Let's go and get drunk somewhere."

Francesca looked up at me, pinching both eyes. I pointed to a girl who was chewing gum, blowing large pink bubbles.

"You don't chew gum," I said, "when you're celebrating the Incarnation of God, the Mystery of Mysteries."

"Shhhh!" she snapped. "People are watching us."

Actually, nobody was watching. It wouldn't matter if we rolled on the floor and got into a wrestling match. The celebrants rambled about, said "Hi", waved, cracked jokes. A few women were combing their hair. A young man fiddled self-consciously with his sleek moustache.

Then the priest appeared, the chorus began to belt out the halleluias, and the High Mass got under way. The rustling and humming and elbowing stopped, the priest climbed into the pulpit, and began his sermon. Short and thin, he spoke with a sharp nasal voice, nodding his bald head, which glittered from the Christmas candles ablaze on the altar.

"Well," he said, peering about at his swollen congregation. "Now whadya suppose it's all about? The business of Christmas."

"You see!" I said to Francesca. "You see how he thinks! *Business!*"

"I'll tell you what it's all about—," he said loudly, "it's Christ in the Manger."

I yawned. But wait—something is going on in front of me. A young man was calmly fondling his girlfriend's behind. He was just doing it, as if he were tweaking his own ear. The girl looked up and smiled seraphically—as the priest wrapped up his sermon.

6

After Mass we made our way gingerly down ice-covered River Road. Glad to be back indoors, we sat down with our coats on. It was going to be a cold night.

I boiled some water for tea. It was time to swap gifts. I forget what Francesca gave me, but whatever it was, I was grateful. Like they say, it's the thought that counts. Well, that is what they say.

I made her tea and gave her my gift. For some reason, her head dropped, and she looked away from me. I recognized the look at once, old weatherman that I was.

"Francesca," I said, "what's the matter?"

Like a lady of stone she sat, her thick sensual mouth tightly closed.

"Don't you like my gift?"

She lowered her head on the table after she sipped some tea. I went to the sofa, sat down, and looked out the window through the curtains. The sky looked frozen—not a trace of Christmas cheer. Another round of futile banter. She might as well go in the other room and get under some warm covers. The room in the back, smaller and windowless, was warmer.

With a long irritated face, she closed the door behind her.

Oh well, I thought to myself, guess I'll have to sleep on the sofa out here. For a long time I sat there, my coat draped over me, looking out the window. The heat now was completely off. The wind blew against the big window facing the river. God! It was cold! By now hardly anyone was outside or on the road. Winter had us in its grip; it was squeezing us hard.

What a way to spend Christmas Eve! I was too numb to feel angry. Being dragged to church, having to watch those kids goose each other while the good priest prattled on about the business of Christmas. For a moment I thought of Padre Pio's Mass, the Mass I missed a decade ago.

The spirit of Christmas was dead inside me. Each year I watched a little more of the old magic fade. This night seemed the end. The afterglow of all my childhood Christmases seemed spent. Not a quiver, not a breath of Yuletide spirit. I looked out the window at stars twinkling in the bowels of godless space—and I dropped into a dreamless sleep.

7

In the morning a voice woke me. I looked up from under my coat. The room was filled with sunlight. Francesca was staring at the plant by the window.

"Look! Look!" she said, "The plant flowered overnight!"

"What?" I grumbled.

"Your plant! Your plant bloomed!"

I got up and walked to the window. Several white buds had appeared at the top of the highest green waxy leaves. My first reaction was to feel pleased. Then I felt puzzled.

I walked around the plant, staring at it in disbelief. The air was fragrant. I bent over and sniffed the white buds. I touched them, softer than infant flesh. Francesca's face had relaxed. Her eyes were laughing. I put my arms around her, and we hugged each other.

I turned toward the plant.

"I just don't get it!"

The small white buds seemed so out of place—so out of time. "Wow!" she said. "Pretty weird!" The sweet smell was intense. The more I thought, the more my feelings were mixed. I didn't know whether to feel grateful or paranoid.

"It's beautiful," Francesca said, taking it all in stride.

"Sure is," I said.

Francesca went to the other room. In a moment, I heard the ethereal tinkle of her piccolo—a riff of fairy music.

We decided to have brunch at the Plaza Diner.

"Shall we go?" I said. Francesca stood over the plant, stroking the fat glossy leaves, sniffing the candy-sweet petals.

"It's a Christmas card from heaven!" she said.

With that we buttoned up and started on our walk to the Diner.

8

The holidays came and went, but I continued to think about my plant and the strange way it blossomed on that abnormally cold Christmas morning. It wasn't normal for a plant like that to bloom in the middle of the winter solstice. And on Christmas morning!

The buds bloomed into full-sized flowers, which I photographed. The smell was overwhelming. A rich, almost-too-sweet fragrance filled every cranny of the apartment. When the petals fell, I gathered them in a box.

I was intrigued by this experience; but it also made me feel uneasy. For a while I tried to explain the plant's behavior as something normal and ordinary, and I could see why some people might feel the compulsion to debunk uncanny occurrences. The anomalous flowering of my plant *felt* unnatural. Especially the sickly sweet perfume. It made me anxious—as if I were losing my grip, getting caught in something beyond my control.

9

Animists are people who say that plants and rivers and stars have souls. An animist might offer the following explanation of Francesca's "Christmas card from heaven."

When the plant bloomed on Christmas morning, it was thanking me for a favor I once did it. The story goes back some. I was living in a loft in Chinatown, a dozen years ago, when I first bought the tropical shrub. It grew big. One summer I left it in the care of students who forgot to water it. It died, but instead of throwing it out, I took care of it.

The plant revived. Years passed. It grew till it was five feet tall. I liked to spritz the giant, and tended the soil. As it got bigger, it became harder to cart around when I moved, which was often. Catless, dogless, wifeless, I nevertheless remained faithful to this plant. I guess you could say we had cultivated a kind of relationship.

According to the animistic story, the plant remembered how once I saved it from death. A basket case, I turned it around, I brought it back to life! So on that Christmas Eve, when I sat forlorn and frozen stiff in Edgewater, New Jersey, my old plant sensed my disconsolate mood, and thought: "He was kind to me once. There now! I'll make my buds bloom! I'll make him think of spring!"

10

Of course, only kids believe in fairy tales. So there must be a more rational explanation. But what? The more I looked into the matter the more puzzling it became; once again I found myself face to face with something I couldn't quite explain.

There were three possibilities.

The first was coincidence—a natural occurrence.

The second was that we—me, Francesca, and the plant—made it flower ourselves. Unconsciously, in a manner unknown to science.

The third possibility was, well—some kind of a miracle. God decided to give a sign, send us a personal message of Christmas cheer. Perhaps to make up for the lousy sermon we had to listen to in Fort Lee. As Francesca said, a Christmas card from heaven!

11

To determine if there was a natural explanation, I researched the habits of my plant. Can a plant of this type bud at such a low temperature?

I knew that plants need warmth and sunlight. I also knew that some plants have odd habits. Night plants like poinsettia, for instance; these beauties need darkness before they can bloom. I speculated. Perhaps the plant had a kind of near-death experience. On the verge of being frozen to death, in a last spasm, it budded; perhaps budding on the verge of death was like the mystic joy dying people experience. I recalled that men sometimes ejaculate at the moment of death— last chance to cast their seed into the womb of time.

I found my plant was of the species *dracaena fragrans,* a tropical shrub that flowered infrequently; it normally requires a tropical climate.

I went to two local florists. Two people in the first said they had *never* seen a dracaena flower. Flowering in bitter cold was beyond what they knew of the plant's habits. And flowering at night was extraordinary, since light is needed to stimulate budding.

The next florist I visited told me a story of his own. A customer once gave him her favorite cactus. She was elderly and too sick to care for it herself. The florist took the plant in, and forgot the woman. About a year passed. One day the cactus produced a beautiful red flower. The woman who gave him the cactus died the same morning.

The story made me uneasy. I worried that my plant flowering was an ill omen. I felt uneasy again when I spoke to an opera lover who told me a strange story. An opera star died one day in winter. Snow had fallen during the night. Near his doorstep on the morning of his death a red rose had bloomed. Beside the rose lay a dead songbird, fallen from the sky.

These weren't stories I wanted to hear. Again I tried to find a natural explanation, talking with experts. A biology professor had nothing to add to what the florists said, except that she thought the whole thing was freaky. Finally, I went to the Bronx Botanical Gardens, and spoke with botanists and seasoned gardeners. Not one of them ever saw a *dracaena fragrans* flower. All agreed that bitter cold and darkness were enemies to tropical plants. One botanist declared it a "miracle."

12

If there is no ordinary explanation, perhaps we should consider the second possibility that we ourselves were the magical engineers who made the plant bloom.

I assume there is a mechanism, a genetic programme, responsible for every plant's reproductive life. Normally, some physical stimulus—heat, water, sunlight—triggers the mechanism. The second possibility is that we ourselves somehow were the "triggers."

Perhaps, to compensate for low spirits, I used my latent psychokinetic power to set the budding into motion. Or perhaps I did it in concert with Francesca's psychokinesis. Of course, we would have "done" all this unwittingly. If this is the correct explanation, it implies a strange picture of what human beings may be capable of doing. It says something about unknown powers of the human soul—unknown instruments and avenues of influence.

13

There is yet the last possibility to consider. Perhaps there is something we have forgotten about sacred time—about holy days and healing times. Maybe the plant's bizarre behavior was caused by something above our individual, tribal, or species mind. By the mind, as some might say, of God. Maybe Francesca was right, and it really was a Christmas card from heaven.

*He resolved to have a moving image of eternity,
and he madethis image revolve according to number, and he let this image be called time.*
                                        Plato, The Timaeus

PART FIVE
OF TIME
AND THE SOUL

We have yet to face the greatest barriers to reclaiming the ancient soul vision: time and death. In this section, we look at time. Time, a root category of being, may seem an enemy to the soul's aspirations.

And yet the soul, even in everyday life, is already busy transcending time. In memory we take hold of the past; in imagination we project into the future.

There are experiences that suggest more exotic abilities of navigating the future. Once again we find ourselves in the realm of dreams; in dreams, it would appear, the soul gains eyes for seeing the far side of time.

Souls cannot ascend without music.
Pythagoras

Chapter Nine

How to Improvise the Music of the Spheres

Our image of time shapes our image of reality. Question the normal image of time, and we question the normal image of reality.

A child is born, becomes a man or woman, grows old, and dies. Time, when it behaves properly, walks in a straight line, unturning, unbending. We never see old men grow back into children. Nor do we watch autumn's yellow leaves return to green or go from dust heaps back upon the branches of trees. We seem fatally in the grips of time marching forward. Time is destiny, straight as an arrow, irreversible.

Nothing is more common than the idea of time. Children learn to tell time, but one might become an old man and never know what time is. Time puzzles the greatest thinkers. Some say time is unreal. Others say it is the soul of the real. Still others claim the puzzles of time are pseudo-puzzles, verbal illusions. Time touches all things—but can you catch the butterfly of time and place it beneath the glass of a clear concept?

Time has many faces. Measurable clock time differs from subjective time, for instance. (Ask anybody waiting for their lover on a street corner.) There is biological time, astronomical time, psychological time. Time that travels in a straight line and time that travels in circles and cycles. There is timing, there is timeliness, and there is timelessness. There is the tempo of music and the kairos of prophecy. There is *illud tempus*, sacred and mythical time. There is the dreamtime of aborigines and the arcane times of tachyons, Relativity Theory, and quantum mechanics.

2

No quirk in time's behavior is as puzzling as precognition. Precognition upsets our normal picture of reality; for it seems to reverse the normal sequence of cause and effect. Suppose I dream an event before it occurs. How could an event that hasn't occurred produce an effect?

Nevertheless, a body of facts shows that weird things in the realm of time do happen. The future does sometimes seem to cast shadows backward into the present.

3

Precognition is so odd—on the face of it, *logically* impossible— that even psychical researchers have doubts. It seems easier to explain precognition by coincidence, by clairvoyance and sub- liminal calculation, or by psychokinesis (PK or mind over matter).

For example, suppose that you dream of some highly particular occurrence that comes true. Instead of saying you precognized it—which puts the effect before the cause—we can say that *you caused the event by PK.* This interpretation disturbs logic less, though it may also lead to incredible conclusions.

For example, suppose I dream of a plane crash before it occurs. If I reject precognition, I could say that I caused the crash by means of a huge burst of psychokinesis (PK). Perhaps there's somebody on the plane I don't like. Such an idea seems as crazy as precogni- tion. No wonder people shy away from these things!

4

Precognition may be psychokinesis in disguise, I once said during a lecture. What looks like anticipating the future may be causing the future. You could take the same fact in two ways: as evidence for precognition *or* psychokinesis.

At hour's end, a woman with a pale face came up to me and shared some troubling experiences. According to the woman, she had the disconcerting ability to foresee peoples' deaths. Worse, she had a knack for previewing the demise of her spouses. Indeed, she had premonitions of her last two husband's deaths.

Her first husband died in an auto wreck; her last from a sudden heart attack. Her recently deceased was driving a car, seemed in good health, but developed chest pains at a busy intersection, and died. A week before, she dreamt he had died at the very street where he met his end. Death, according to the frazzled lady, occurred within a month after her dream.

My point about psychokinesis made her wonder. Could she somehow have caused the death of the men in her life? PK, I repeated, was only a logical possibility.

"I have a new friend," she said. "He was my husband's partner. He wants to look after me. He says that's how Jim would've wanted it. But I'm afraid. What if it happens again?"

I told her not to hold herself responsible, that her dreams were probably coincidental. Still, I felt a twinge of concern for the lady's new friend. It was the last I ever saw of her.

5

One telltale sign is a dream that repeats itself—like a messenger that keeps knocking on the door. Three times, for instance, I dreamt of fire, explosion, dead bodies. I saw charred corpses, laid out in rows on the street. An explosion from below, a boiler or gas tank.

We're going to hear about a big fire, I proclaim rather confidently to several people. About a week later, front page pictures of dead bodies, lined up in rows on the street; a boiler in a Kentucky hotel exploded, causing a killer fire.

6

There is another type of dream—a mixture of a precognitive and great dream. In such dreams a trend of one's soul life is foreshadowed—a new direction heralded, a new horizon of possibilities. A *prophetic* dream. In a prophetic dream, the precognitive element is couched in symbols. A symbol points beyond the personal to the transpersonal.

I met Swami Nadabrahmananda in April, 1976. Famous in India as a master of a rare yoga of sound, I knew right away I was in the presence of an extraordinary man.

The building on 24rd Street, in Manhattan, looked rundown. On the door of the old brownstone were inscribed four words: *Serve, Love, Meditate, Realize.* I removed my shoes, and followed a sign pointing upstairs: "This Way For Music Students."

"Michael?" Nada said when I knocked. (His students called him Nada or Swami Nada.

"I wasn't sure if I should knock."

"No, no," he said warmly. "This is your time."

At once he sounded the theme of time. It was my time. I had arrived at the right time and this very time was reserved for me.

"Come, Michael," he said, pointing to a place beside him. A bald brown head with brown piercing eyes nodded. His arms were soft and smooth; his belly protruding. I looked around at the walls:

everywhere pictures of Swami Sivananda, the famed doctor turned guru. The air was sweet with incense.

Not chance but action from a previous life led me to his feet, Nada said. My time with him was part of a timeless pattern. He used his favorite metaphor: "All on film," he said. He added that I and generations of my offspring could now achieve *moksha* — liberation from the cycle of death and rebirth.

"Swami Nada," I said at once, "I dreamt a strange dream some time before I met you. I dreamt I was sailing in a boat. Nobody knew where we were going, but suddenly a man appeared, a very old and funny man. The man—he looked like you—gave me a music lesson."

Nada lowered his eyes.

"The man in the dream said only one thing to me: 'There will be no instruments.'"

I stopped a moment, uncertain if he understood me. Nada's English was weak.

"You see," I went on, "I already have a music teacher—a flute teacher. A few days later a friend called and told me about you." I looked squarely at him: "Did you pay me a visit from the future?"

He just looked at me and nodded. Nada was eighty-one but the portly monk had a baby face, soft unwrinkled skin. His eyes were kindly and penetrating. The lines in the palm of his left hand were star-shaped, as if by design. Resting his hand in mine, he allowed me to inspect it; it seemed weightless.

"Mind control is life," he then pronounced, adding with majestic simplicity: "Rhythm is music."

7

Talk, of course, was not Nada's specialty. He was a sound man, a music man, and his teaching went back through millennia of oral tradition. Like Pythagoras, master of the living mathematics we call music, Nada used numbers for learning what he called "mind control" and "rhythm." The meditative ordering of vital energies, the consecration of breath itself, was the essence of the sacred for him. The way into the circle of sacred time was simple and unpretentious. A child's game—counting!

He demonstrated *tala keherawa*—four beats. A mudra in time, he clapped on the first beat, each succeeding one tapped a different finger on the palm of the opposing hand, beginning with his pinky.

"One, two, three, four," he slowly intoned. A wave of calm rolled over me. He looked at me as if I were a child taking the first lessons in the beat of eternal life. His voice rumbled softly, like an etheric mountain stream. He doubled the tempo. *Dhagi, natin, naka, dhina.*

Again. Like a stream bubbling, rushing over pebbles, syllables slurred to infinite velocity.

"Count!" he said, beckoning me to join him. The thought of doing a duet with the song man of the universe jarred me. I clapped at the wrong beat. He stopped and chuckled: "What you thinking then?"

Each time I made a mistake: back to the beginning—slowly, slowly, slowly.

"Full mind need," he said.

8

To spend time with Nadabrahmananda I had to take music lessons. Music was Nada's spiritual practice, his *sadhana*. He didn't preach or philosophize. His entire spiritual life was based on music.

Once the court musician for the king of Mysore, in the upheavals of Indian politics, he was cast adrift. He went to the mountains, intending to kill himself; wild animals befriended him. The great Swami Sivananda found and commandeered him into monkhood.

Nada never ate meat or married. A *ghandarva*—a celestial musician—he practiced, played, and taught music constantly. Nada's name means "intelligible sound" or "divine breath." His life mirrored his name. Always in tune with himself, wherever he went and whatever he did, he hummed, pulsed, vibrated. In some way, at some level, he was always making music.

9

Nada picked up a small harplike instrument called a *swarmandala*, or *sky-ship*. Casually, he strummed. It seemed, as I listened, that I heard echoes of what Pythagoras called the monochord, the sound said to transport a soul to the Seventh Heaven. According to an ancient writer on music, Aristides Quintilianus, Pythagoras on his deathbed asked to hear the monochord.

"Souls cannot ascend without music," he is supposed to have said. Ancient soulmakers, especially the Pythagoreans, had a high regard for music. At the end of his life Socrates had a change of heart about music.

10

In the *Phaedo,* which describes his last conversation on earth, Socrates says:

"In the course of my life I have often had intimations in dreams that I should compose music. The same dream came to me sometimes in one form, and sometimes in another, but always saying the same or nearly the same words: 'Cultivate and make music,' said the dream."

Socrates always thought he was making music, for to his mind philosophy was the greatest music. But the dream kept returning, troubling his nights in prison, making him think about his imminent journey to the "other place."

The great dialectician wondered if there was something he was supposed to do. Maybe the dream meant him to make music—to really make music. Perhaps he was being called to make amends to the Muses. Socrates, who esteemed the gods of his tribe, heeded his dream. So, as we are told in the *Phaedo,* he set the fables of Aesop to verse.

11

Socrates deathbed dream about making music speaks to soul-makers. Philosophy—without art, without music—isn't enough. The fullness of soul life calls for the cooperation of both brain hemispheres.

Cultivate and make music—while studying philosophy I kept having dreams with the same message.

I'm riding on top of a train, holding on to a cord. I bob up and down as the train moves, like a balloon on a string. The string drops from my hand, and I float up into the sky, above a dark house. Night changes into dawn, and up into the sky I soar, in a rapture of freedom. Down below I can see violet-colored lakes, calm as glass, and a fantastic forest of shimmering emerald. Riding on a gleaming silver flute, I sail through the open sky.

12

I'm looking across a narrow inlet in a bay. Pitch black. Then a knife of golden light rips open the sky. I meet an unknown woman by the shore. She scoops out of the sand a small carmine music-case. Inside, a little flute, not quite as small as a piccolo, shines with a golden light. I lift it to my lips, but can't make a sound.

The beach is deserted, and I feel stupid, unable to get a sound from my magic flute. Then the wizard of jazz flute, Hubert Laws, appears.

"It's there," he says.

I raise the flute to my lips. I look at him, pursing my lips.

Again, the Master says: "IT'S THERE."

I blow a soft breath into the blow-hole, and to my amazement, a great burly sound floats out, making the beach reverberate with cascades of thunder. Like a summer storm, the sound blows out to sea, echoing over the waters, fading over the horizon.

13

For a moment I had a clear sense of being a master of my instrument. The secret was total effortlessness, fused with total concentration. For an instant I knew what it felt like to improvise the music of the spheres.

In the midst of studying philosophy, I kept dreaming about the flute. What did it mean? Was I supposed to become a musician? Or was I to try to restore the soul of the Muses to philosophy, search for a new harmonics of soul and reason? Hadn't Pythagorean science striven to fuse magic, music, and mathematics? The great Renaissance scientists, like Kepler and Copernicus, were still inspired by this holistic vision. There were traces of Pythagoras in Galileo and Newton, although after these giants, science and philosophy went the way of soulless mechanism.

Already at the source of our tradition, Socrates on his deathbed understood that something was amiss. Our intellect, to complete itself, to make itself worthy of life's greatest challenges, needs to unite with the soul of music.

14

The man in my dream said "no instruments." What did that mean? For one thing, Swami literally used his own body as an instrument for making music. He was a master of *thaans,* wordless vibrations that echo notes of the *raga,* the melodic form. In classical Indian music, first the notes are sung, *sa, ri, ga.* . . , then *ah, ah, ah* . . . the vibrations are hummed. Every song begins this way, first the *raga,* then the *thaan.* Nada directed these vibrations to different parts of his body, especially to his spinal cord. It stimulated his vital centers and energies. He began with long internal vibrations, barely audible. Slowly, a sound would materialize from deep inside his body.

"You see," he said, "each of the *chakras* I control every day in my *sadhana.* Called *kundalini thaans.* " Scientists from several countries confirmed the *kundalini thaan* vibrations in his spinal cord.

"Experiment, three men hold me—vibration coming here!"

He pointed to his spinal cord. A microphone placed by his coccyx registered the effects of a subtle musical vibration. Nada was a human vibrator, an instrument for transmitting divine energy.

There is no instrument, said the dream: We ourselves are the instruments. In Nada Yoga our bodies—our living souls—are instruments for making divine music.

My dream "came" true in another sense. Nada stressed freedom, flexibility. Every place and every situation is an opportunity to make music. You can practice anywhere—even "in the latrine"— he liked to say. You can count, hum, chant the divine names anywhere.

Nada, like Hubert Laws and John Coltrane, was a master improvisor. Jazz and Nada Yoga have this in common; they are arts of improvisation. So, it's not that there isn't any instrument, but that everything is an instrument—the essence of improvisation.

Nada told me a story about the flute. Lord Krishna, wandering through the forest, found a plain bamboo flute with six holes. Each of the holes represents a human passion: desire, jealousy, ambition, anger, and so forth—the dark soul energies. When Lord Krishna played his bamboo flute, he "played" with all these dark energies, using them to lift his soul to God.

The point was clear: the sacred way to "play the flute" is to make use of life's problems and obstacles. The worst stuff that life has to throw at us, as Keats implied, was grist for soulmaking; everything depends on how you use your instrument—and your main "instrument" is your life.

15

Nada Yoga, said the Swami, was perfect for people living during the Kaliyuga—the present dark age of the spirit.

Kaliyuga—the age of Kali—the time of disintegration. In short, endtime, apocalypse. According to Nada, the sign of this apocalyptic Kaliyuga is collective "mental uncontrol," and the proof is that people are constantly fighting.

Ours is an age of information without heart, he often said. Loss of memory was loss of soul. Nada knew hundreds of ragas by heart. His was an oral tradition—a tradition of heart.

Nada's mind moved in memories of time. He knew nothing of clocks; he was his own clock. With him everything was based on inner timing, being in tune with an older, more rhythmic time consciousness. Drum, chant and harmonium were his ways of tuning into that other time consciousness.

In the dark age of spirit—in the Kaliyuga—music is the best discipline for soulmakers. The reason is simple: Music is a direct appeal to the heart—a direct sounding of the living breath. The yoga of sound Nada practiced was a science of the divine pleasure principle. Use the chance to make divine music, he often said, or suffer incarnation over and over again. For some reason, he was afraid of being reincarnated as a pig, a creature he especially disliked.

16

Swami Nada never dreamed. Scientists in India, Europe, Canada, and the United States tested him for REM sleep several nights running; they found no evidence that he dreamed.

I asked him why he never dreamed.

"No desires," he said. "I always chant the Divine Name."

That was his sole aim in life, the sole quest of the *ghandarva,* the musician of the etheric spheres. This made for a cheerfully detached view of life. Good and bad were "the same," the old man often said: We come into the world empty and we leave empty. Only the divine name abides—the divine song.

Through time Nadabramanda had mastered time. His being was an echo from a timeless song world of soul ragas. He was always on time. And he was timeless. I was lucky to remember him from the future.

*Everything that ever has meant anything
has just as truly meant something else.*
Charles Fort
Wild Talents

Chapter Ten
The Secret Assassin

Late afternoon, March 30, 1981, I received a phone call from a friend. The voice at the other end of the line was shaking. It said: "You were right! The President was shot!"

That afternoon, John W. Hinckley, Jr., attempted to assassinate President Ronald Reagan. I was shocked, but not totally, for in the last month, I had three times dreamt that the President was shot. The dreams made an uncanny impression on me, and I wrote them down, and shared them with the friend that phoned.

"He's not dead."

"No."

"He won't die. He's going to be all right."

The moment I heard what happened, I felt sure he'd recover.

2

February 13, I wrote in my notebook: "Dreamt the President was shot. Left shoulder. Then he goes down."

February 25: "Another dream about the President. Shot. Goes down. Noise, confusion, people running about."

March 12: "Dreamt of President Reagan. Third time now. He's stripped from the waist up. He looks younger than usual; he radiates health."

3

The information in the three dreams added up to this. The President was shot, he was shot in the left shoulder, and he would recover. The last point was shown symbolically in the last dream: I saw the President, looking youthful, his body in fine shape.

As we know, President Reagan was indeed shot. A bullet had indeed lodged in his left side, penetrating his lung. And indeed the

President did not die, the doctors remarking, as reported in The New York Times, on his "amazing" recovery. The number of details, though small, were all important. Most striking, for me, was that the dream repeated itself three times. The second dream contained no new imagery; it repeated the message of the assassination attempt. The third dream comments on the outcome of the first two; the image of a man who triumphs over fate came through.

To talk here of coincidence seems implausible. Three dreams that zero in on the same idea don't look coincidental to me. On the face of it, it looks like a case of precognition.

4

Let's consider the facts more closely. First of all, as in other foreshadowing episodes of mine, this one involved matters I was, at the time, deeply interested in, matters that were absorbing my attention. My foreshadowing dream of Swami Nadabrahmananda, for example, seemed an offshoot of my interest in music at that time.

About the time of the attempted assassination, the President and his policies were on my mind. In particular, I (like other uneasy observers) was focused on the worsening nuclear arms race.

The following is a rough account of the thoughts I was having about the President at the time. Might there be some evolutionary meaning in the growing nuclear arms crisis? I wondered. Several ideas, fantastic at first glance, had gradually installed themselves in my mind. I had come to believe that the nuclear arms race—then being stirred up by the President's bellicose rhetoric—was the logical outgrowth of a specific way of constructing reality in the Western world. The Bomb seemed less an accidental development but the logical conclusion of a certain worldview.

From Thales to Teller, I saw a single line of development. I saw the Bomb as a symbol of closure for Western science, the endpoint, the dead end past which we could go no further. The Bomb, I began to suspect, might be providing a stimulus, a spur perhaps, to the evolution of human consciousness. Something extreme was needed, a return, a rediscovery of the forgotten Pythagorean tradition, of ideals of harmony with nature, of the unlived feminine in the collective soul. If there was a Mind at Large guiding the evolution of the species, it might well be using the Bomb as a device to force us to mobilize our evolutionary potential.

The Bomb was the perfect vehicle for acting out certain age-old obsessions of Judeo-Christian eschatology. It is now known that astrology played a part in the Reagan Administration. But the interest in things psychic and spiritual goes back much further. For instance, in October, 1970, Ronald Reagan held a seance in the Governor's Mansion with his wife, Nancy, Pat Boone, Herbert Ellingwood, and preachers Harold Bredesen and George Otis. A spirit "spoke" to Reagan through the voice of Otis: "You will reside at 1600 Pennsylvania." (Reported August 6, 1984, in *Newsweek*.) The President was evidently open to people who took stock in spirits. (The "spirit" apparently scored a hit.)

The President has shown more than a passing interest in biblical prophecy. For example, according to a report tape-recorded by Los Angeles *Times* reporter, Robert Scheer, Reagan said to Jerry Falwell in 1981: "Jerry, I believe we're heading very fast for Armageddon right now." The President made many statements like this.

Surrounded by Pat Boone and Jerry Falwell, fundamentalist believers in the apocalypse, the President seemed to be setting the stage for a "countdown to Armageddon"—big televangelist buzzwords. He was doing this by demonizing the Soviet Union as the *focus of evil.*

But, I wondered, whose side was the President really on? So good-natured and gently winning in his outward manner, Ronald Reagan seemed a fine candidate for the role of Antichrist in this pending world drama. According to the myth, Antichrist isn't a blatantly wicked figure. Antichrist doesn't come on belching sulphur and dripping gore. That sort of thing belongs in grade-B horror flicks. Antichrist disguises himself under the appearance of good. It's the only way it can gain a foothold on the world stage. Antichrist doesn't operate by frontal attack but by disinformation and counterfeit.

Of course, I didn't believe that Ronald Reagan was literally the Antichrist; but he did seem to have the right qualities—or lack of qualities—for playing into the hands of demonic forces. Like Eichmann, I thought in an unkind moment, his banality made him a tool for an evil of grand proportions.

Such, at any rate, were my thoughts about the President just before the attempt on his life. It is at least possible that my recent, novel, and intense interest in his career may have psychically sensitized me to perils that lay in store for him.

5

And yet perhaps this wasn't a case of precognition at all. There are other possibilities—but first some facts about the failed assassin, the third party to this bizarre paranormal triangle.

Blue-eyed, sandy-haired John Hinckley was the son of a Denver oil executive. His parents were devout Christians, but Hinckley lived in the shadow of dominant siblings. A quiet, ordinary boy, he became more aggressive as he grew older, dabbling in neo-Nazism. But even his Nazi cohorts thought him unstable, and he was expelled from the National Socialist Party of America. A junk-food addict, an amateur guitarist, Hinckley also tried his hand at writing. Before the assassination attempt, the twenty-five year old had been wandering aimlessly around the country. He quit college, took odd jobs, and saw himself as a failure.

Hinckley drifted into fantasizing about Jodie Foster, then a teenaged actress, who plays a prostitute in *Taxi Driver*. In the 1978 movie, Robert De Niro plays an alienated ex-marine, Travis Bickle, who plans to assassinate a United States Senator and befriends a twelve year old prostitute. After botching the assassination, Bickle goes on the rampage in a seedy New York hotel, where he kills a pimp and somehow ends up hailed as a hero.

The movie apparently inflamed Hinckley's imagination. He began to write love letters to Jodie Foster, and sent her his poetry. It must have made Hinckley feel romantic to imagine himself killing a powerful leader; if he did such a thing, surely he would count in people's eyes. Aren't strong men idolized by beautiful women? The idea of assassinating the President apparently grew from watching the movie.

It's a case of fact imitating fiction. A piece of acting inspires Hinckley to try to kill the President—himself an ex-actor.

But this crisscrossing back and forth between dream and reality, fantasy and fact, has another odd twist. Paul Schrader's screenplay for *Taxi Driver* mirrors the diaries of Arthur Bremen, who shot and paralyzed George Wallace in Laurel, Maryland, 1972, where Wallace was campaigning to be president. According to Schrader, his screenplay was written before the diaries came out. He was surprised by the likeness between Bremen's diary and what he wrote.

What was going on there? Was it that the image of assassination was in the air? Or do these images wander around on the back roads of Mind at Large, and seek each other out by the law of affinity, and thus add pressure toward making them come true?

History! What a strange web of fact and fiction, reality and fantasy! Artist, actor, assassin, politician—our deeds and our dreams play off each other in subtle, uncanny ways.

Perhaps uncannier than we think.

Hinckley had purchased a .22 caliber revolver from Rocky's Pawn Shop in Dallas. Rocky's? What made him pick a place with a name like that? Was it sympathy with another loser who takes a wild chance and wins—Rocky Balboa? Rocky, the Sylvester Stallone character: underdog, comer up from nowhere, heavyweight champion of the world!

An hour and a half before he shot the President, Hinckley drafted a letter—which he never mailed—to Jodie Foster. In this letter he admits he wanted to impress the young actress. Jodie Foster never answered his love letters, but Hinckley had the courage of desperation. There was still a way to make up for this spurned love, still a way to impress the girl of his dreams: Why not kill the President of the United States? She'd have to stand up and notice him, if he killed the most powerful man on earth.

6

But now the puzzle is how this twisted stuff of murderous ambition found its way into *my* mind. Any way I try to answer this question forces me to rearrange my ideas of how the world works. Precognition, if a fact of nature, probably implies the most drastic revisions. However, there are some slightly less drastic ways of dealing with my apparent precognition of the attempted assassination.

Telepathy, for example. The police found that Hinckley was planning the assassination for a while. Exactly how long and how definite his intentions were, we'll never know for sure. He may have only vaguely and indecisively toyed with the idea, but then finally acted on impulse. Suppose the scheme was in his head for weeks or months; I may have divined by telepathy his plan to shoot the President. This might seem to make the hypothesis of precognition unnecessary.

In that case, I have two questions. First, why should I—out of billions of possible people—have been telepathically attuned to Hinckley's plan? Second, and more damning to the hypothesis of telepathy: Even if I did pick up Hinckley's murderous plan telepathically, the precise *outcome* of the attempt on the President's life would have remained unknown to me.

Shot in the *left shoulder.* That's fairly precise. He might have missed, or shot Reagan in the toe. He might have maimed or killed him. It's hard to see how I could subliminally calculate, even assuming unusual clairvoyant powers, the inherently unpredictable outcome of such an event.

Odds against me being the person with whom Hinckley would telepathically resonate were billions to one. Was there something that favored this wild "coincidence"? One possibility is this. Perhaps at some level of my being I felt an unconscious sympathy with Hinckley. For instance, I might have sympathized with his plight as a drifter—a confused, aimless young man. Perhaps this unconscious sympathy—which I postulate purely for the sake of argument—attuned me to Hinckley's plans.

7

Now consider a darker speculation: I might have been in sympathy with John Hinckley's plan to kill the President. Needless to say, I would never consciously entertain the wish to kill the President. However, my conscious morality is no guarantee against the immoral tendencies of my unconscious. If we have learned anything from Sigmund Freud, it is the huge gap between the morality of consciousness and the immorality of the unconscious.

A man as powerful as the President of the United States is likely to awaken in more than one soul the ungodly will to murder. We are not masters in our house; our unconscious minds harbor forbidden wishes, which are often much at odds with the manners and mores of humane society. Almost any powerful person who occupies a prominent place in public consciousness is likely to attract a mass of more or less unconscious hostility. In the metaphor of the Chinese philosopher, Chuang Tzu—the tallest tree attracts the lightning-bolt!

This leads to the second (and weirder) possibility. Perhaps my apparent precognition was really a subtle form of psychokinesis. Instead of passively foreseeing the event, I may have unconsciously helped to bring it about. (I spoke of this possibility in regard to the lady who kept precognizing her husbands' deaths.)

This is a strange idea, of course, with even stranger implications. Certainly, it is dismaying to think we may have such clandestine power. The possibility of unconscious destructive PK makes me feel rather vulnerable, and I am therefore reluctant to admit it really exists.

The implications for everyday life are unnerving. One might wonder how many of our misfortunes are brought about by our neighbor's insidious PK. And what of the ill will that too often secretly festers in the unconscious minds of our intimate friends and relations? Throughout human history the power of witches, warlocks, and sorcerers has been acknowledged, feared, and proscribed. Once we admit the existence of our destructive PK potential, we would have to widen our worldview to include many nasty possibilities rationalism was supposed to have banished to the limbo of superstition.

8

It is, of course, hard to imagine how this secret assassin—our murderous PK potential—would actually work. Consider the following very rough model. Let us, for the sake of argument, assume that an intention to injure the President existed in the minds of a critical mass of people at some unconscious level.

We could then think of Hinckley becoming a kind of temporary robot or golem, a machine for carrying out these unconscious impulses. Think of all the hostile impulses seething in the shadow of the collective soul, directed against the supreme authority: All these would provide a vast labile system, psychically disposed to wreak havoc on the target—in this case, the President of the United States.

What we need now is a properly excited "electron," one that this collective force can kick into the orbit of violent crime.

Let me explain something about instability and psychokinesis. Experimental studies show that psychokinesis works on dice that are in motion, that are, so to speak, unstable with regard to their momentum in space. It is harder to dislodge a die sitting at rest by PK; in the experimental setup, you roll the dice, and try to influence them while they tumble indeterminately in space. It might work the same way with people.

From what is known of his life and character, Hinckley could be described as fluctuating, the psychic equivalent of an excited electron, or a die in motion. A creature of instability and indetermination, he drifted in a world of dreams. He struggled with feelings of aimlessness, of wanting power, and of desperately needing love while feeling unworthy of it. Hinckley operates by suggestion, by slippery associations, *as in a dream.* In a movie house, he watches a pretty girl go with an assassin. He strums on his guitar, but his sound is not full. He dreams some more, still floundering, derelict of clear aim.

His brain is firing, chaotically, excitedly; his thoughts fly, like dice tumbling in space, like excited electrons disposed to jump into new orbits. Meanwhile, as we said, there are impulses wandering, so to speak, on telepathic breezes, fluid and unbound by space. They find a crack in Hinckley, a sluice to pour themselves in. Hinckley would thus become a kind of a psychic "electron" moving at random, and used by the critical mass of collective hostility as an instrument for attempting to assassinate the President.

9

I can picture such a massive unconscious tendency, pushing to realize itself, straining to find an appropriate outlet—if not in Hinckley, then in some other being, some other chink in the President's armor against fate.

However, I'm still puzzled as to how *I* apparently had the outcome of the assassination attempt in mind. My "knowing" the random details of the outcome in this case doesn't support the psychokinetic interpretation of my precognitive dream.

In any case, further oddities arise if we press the PK interpretation of precognition. Let us assume that I "knew" the future in the sense that I willed it; that is, I "knew" that the President would be the target of an assassination attempt, because I unconsciously wished him dead.

If I wished it, am I also guilty? Should we invoke some psychic law of parties? Many a man has suffered capital punishment as a result of being a party to a crime. The guilt is distributed according to intent, not only according to deed. Given the theoretical potency of our most intense thoughts, shouldn't we question our complacent ethics?

The possibility of unconscious group PK raises some odd questions. For instance, should we assume responsibility for our wishes? Are we responsible for our unconscious desires? Did all those who bore ill will toward the President actually try, in some important but subtle way, to kill him?

Peter Abelard, the medieval philosopher, argued that the essence of evil lies in our intentions. Or, to be exact, in the consent we give to our evil desires. Abelard, who had much experience in these matters, was thinking of the saying in Matthew, (5:28): "If a man looks at a woman lustfully, he has already committed adultery with her in his heart." Once we bring PK into the picture, Abelard's fantastic ethics of intention takes on new meaning.

10

It seems that by denying precognition, we may be driven to believe we have strange powers of psychokinesis. On the other hand, if we accept precognition, we are driven to the slippery precipice of logic. The picture we get of our secret soul powers is riddled with uncertainty and ambiguity.

It is as though the artificer of the world wants to keep our minds permanently open, permanently puzzled: perhaps a way of reminding us that the meaning of things can be no more fixed than a child's view through a kaleidoscope. Yet all this may be wrong, and somewhere in the soul of being, all the puzzles will one day vanish, like waves on a calm sea.

*There is beyond this another kind of body,
that is forever attached to the soul, of a celestial
nature, and for this reason everlasting, which
they call radiant or starlike.*
                                    Philoponus the Neoplatonist

PART SIX
SOUL FLIGHT

The boundaries of soul in time are fuzzy. A part of our souls apparently spills over the immediate present of our clock-bound existence. A similar fuzziness is true of the soul in space.

The ancients spoke of soul travel—and indeed the human soul yearns to fly. It's in our blood: this craving to soar, to be released from gravity's grip. We have invented flying machines—why not soul flight? There are, in fact, well documented stories of out-of-body experiences (OBES).

My own experiences have convinced me that human beings have a soul-like power to transcend the body. Certain facts suggest we are not essentially tied to our bodily existence; special circumstances make release possible. Thwarted love or impending death—the immediate causes vary—but there are times when people seem able to escape the prison of the body.

The stories of soul travel I recount complement each other. In the first, it was I—or some aspect of myself—who somehow fled my body and touched another body, three thousand miles away. I wasn't conscious, however, of being "out" during the experience.

The second case was different. The out-of-body caller *was* conscious of being present at the OB location. The setup was quasi-experimental—to be exact, a response to a dare. The effect of these, and related incidents, has been to widen my vision of the possibilities of love and death. For soulmakers, what could be more heartening?

All dreams of the soul end
in a beautiful man's or woman's body.
William Butler Yeats

Chapter Eleven

Trans-Atlantic Astral Sex: A PSI-Rated Story

I was bumming rides across Germany. An Austrian geology professor picked me up, and explained the origin of the Alps as we crossed over them. After a long drive (lunch included), he dropped me at a godforsaken intersection, nine miles from Cologne. Dumped on an island flanked by bushy hillocks, it was getting dark and raining.

A beat-up Mercedes skidded to a stop and another vagabond came tumbling out. Two of us now, we raised our thumbs, hoping for a lift to the next town. By now it was totally dark and we were invisible, except when headlights flashed on us, huddled under our rain jackets.

The Canadian spoke rhapsodically of her lover back home. She missed him so much and could see him in her mind's eye. We curled up under shrubbery between lanes, and wrapped ourselves in our jackets. The rain thinned to a drizzle, fog dampened our faces, and we slept a little.

When daylight came, we got a ride to the airport, drank coffee, and went our ways. The Canadian gave me a phone number in London. Call, she said.

2

When I got to London I phoned. The moment I mentioned the Canadian, I was invited to stay at Hampstead Heath, a lush London suburb.

I discussed Sartre and the Vietnam war with Bernard. David came home late from his job, puffy-eyed, dishevelled, and dejected at how "fatigued" he felt after "imbibing and having sexual inter-course." I stayed over a month at the house on Hampstead Heath. The best part was getting to know Windy.

A native of Australia, Windy was a slim fair-skinned woman of twenty-six—and very genteel. She came from Queensland. Her father was a man of impeccably self-contained manners; he never raised his voice or uttered a profanity. Windy was a world-traveler but the place that intrigued and repelled her most was New York City. New York was the antipodes of the world she grew up in, so it was easy to entertain her with stories of life in the Big Apple. We swapped tales of our travels and, there being nothing to prevent us, fell into the altered state of consciousness known as love.

3

Time, of course, shot by. We hopped round the pubs of Hampstead Heath; went to town for a stroll on Picadilly Circus; took in a play by Oscar Wilde. Toward summer's end, it got cool, and we spent nights indoors.

I'd have stayed on indefinitely, but I had to fly back to New York. As our last days shrank to hours, we began to feel sad about having to part. I stayed a month in Hampstead Heath, and Windy and I enjoyed many carefree and lovely hours together.

Windy saw me to the airport. It seemed we'd known each other for years. We held hands silently as the taxi approached the flight terminal. No talk of plans. I declared I'd miss our night walks on the heath. At the gate before boarding, we kissed and said goodbye. The stage was set for enchantment.

4

Back on Thompson Street in Greenwich Village, I began to miss Windy. Love letters flew back and forth across the Atlantic. I wanted badly to return to London, but it was impossible. Maybe Windy would come to New York. She'd been to New York once before. I wrote trying to persuade her to come. She had no ties in London, liked to travel, and didn't care much for her job.

So she started to save money for the plane fare. The more I thought about seeing Windy again, the more animated I became. When all it has to feed on are pleasant memories—and what can be more pleasant than romance in a foreign country?—love has a way of thriving.

I missed touching her, I missed hearing her voice, I missed looking into her eyes. The soul stuff deep inside me yearned for her.

Our letters got longer. Each sentence we wrote was like a hand that reached out. Our letters were exercises in passionate imaginings. To close the space between us, we wrote detailed descriptions of our daily doings.

I described the damp gloomy evenings—it was a rainy fall—how I moped around, lovesick among the crowds of MacDougal Street and Father Demo Square: I painted verbal pictures for Windy of the hobos, the street musicians, the dope peddlers in Washington Square Park. I wrote about the furious-looking man who marched up and down Eighth Street, dressed like an Elizabethan clown; the beggar who sported a monkey in a tuxedo; the philosophical drunks on Third Avenue; the endless ragtag oddities of Greenwich Village street life. We touched and fondled each other with hands and fingers of words, stretching our feelings across the Atlantic ocean.

In one letter, Windy described a strange experience. It seemed the old house on Hampstead Heath was haunted—of all things—by a dog! One day she climbed up into the attic and was mopping the floor. She looked up and saw a dog sitting next to an old wooden chest—a large golden retriever. The dog looked radiant; it was *smiling* at her. For a split second, Windy—fond of our four-legged friends—stared at the apparition. She realized there was no dog in the house, no way a dog could have gotten in the attic. She screamed, and the apparition turned into a wisp of golden smoke.

5

Windy wasn't the sort to invent wild stories, and reading her account made me want to see her even more.

Before long she'd be flying to New York. The tension that accompanies expectation kept building. Months had passed—so much time, so much space between us! As the days passed Windy's face faded to a pale image in my memory. This image, laced with yearning and twined with expectation, was all I had of her.

6

One day she telephoned from Hampstead Heath. A glitch with her visa was going to delay arrival, and she'd have to come through Canada. That meant waiting not days but weeks, if not months.

It was the last Saturday before Christmas, and New York was manic with consumerism when I got this disappointing news. The lights, the bustle, the mirth of the city seemed empty without the prospect of Windy's arrival. There wasn't much I could do to relieve my discontent.

I tried to visualize her sitting on the couch. I sat down there and put my hands on the window panes, staring sourly up at the New

York sky. Impulsively I got up and shot down the six flights, joined the march of pedestrians on Sixth Avenue, and let myself sink into a romantic depression. After a bowl of Yankee bean soup in a Jewish Deli on Second Avenue, I went back west on Eighth, stopped before the Art Moviehouse, looked at the harried faces of shoppers streaming by, then dragged myself home to Thompson Street.

It was a bad night. Apart from being lovesick, I had to deal with a crackpot artist who lived above me. His apartment was hopping with cats, dogs, monkeys, and a rainbow-colored parrot. Joe, in love with all things primitive, was determined to cram the garden of Eden into his tiny apartment. He, his beasts, and his wife, were having a party. The monkeys were on the rampage, the cats were freaking out, and Joe and Mercy were making merry.

Finally I got into bed, and pushed aside the window curtain. A car screeched and a woman yelled. It was nearly 2 o'clock. Things upstairs had quieted down. Wind scooped the last clouds away and a few stars glinted dully in the sky. I turned from the Manhattan skyline, and began to picture Windy in my mind's eye.

7

The more vividly I pictured her, soaked with the warm memories of those not too far off days, the harder her absence dug into me, like a thorn in my side. I conjured a wisp of her presence. An image of her appeared before me—her fair skin covered with beads of sweat—which quickly melted away.

Nothingness! What a powerful incentive to create! Again I conjured her by the power of my inner eye: She uncoiled herself, standing in yellow-sandalled feet. She leaned her face toward me, pressing the balls of her fingers on my chest. Her skin smelled of the fall heath. Her bird-soft hair brushed my neck. Her voice sounded in my ears.

The image opened like sunflower petals at the kiss of dawn. It reached out and draped itself on me, unfolding into something solid, something weighty; then it receded and stood in the shadows, elusive as a patch of rainbow in a stormy sky.

This way; no, that way. There now! Hold still!

Partly inventing, partly recollecting, I rearrange her: Her perfect calf appears on the blue-and-yellow bed-quilt, fretted with a beam of cold English moonlight. Now her disembodied voice calls from the bathroom. Her feet pad toward me, pale ankles aglow from two candles on the oak night-table. Nearly in bed now, aroused by a slithery extension of once real sensations, a lingering presence, connected by fibers drawn thinly in time.

The tantalizing clarity of the image, faintly fleshed out, quavering on the edge of reality, arouses me and at the same time causes discomfort in my abdomen.

For a while I'm drawn into this spiral of frustration and hallucination, until she is breathing beside me, her sea-green eyes burning with loving looks.

Then, a curious slippage, an increase in velocity. Here, hard to describe, I switch into a strange gear. I stretch soon-ness into now-ness; taking time and space into my own hands, twisting them, molding them, shaping them according to my desire.

I felt I was about to cross a certain boundary—about to shapeshift myself into a creature of pure feeling, a kind of werewolf with good intentions. I was above the laws of profane time and space. I threw my whole being into the bright abyss of my lover's image: In a spasm of spirit, I let go of myself and rose untethered toward the lucid phantasm of her face. Far out I traveled, out on the windy night-sky, across the Atlantic.

8

I stress the intensity of the image—charged with emotion, memories, pent up desires. It may be worth noting in any attempt to account for the sequel. Several days later, I received the following letter from Windy.

9

Dear Michael,

I'm writing this in haste before I go to work. A strange thing happened to me this morning. It was Sunday morning, about eight o'clock. I was lying in bed, half-awake, wishing I didn't have to get up. In the back of my mind, I kept thinking I had to go to the loo, but I didn't move. I was somewhere between sleeping and waking, when it happened. Believe me, I'm not crazy, and my life's not so miserable, that I have to make stories up. But the truth is, suddenly you were in bed with me. You were there! Making love to me! I knew it was you, I couldn't see, but I knew it was you. I felt your body, recognized your voice. I knew I wasn't asleep, it wasn't a dream. I would appreciate it, philosopher, if you would explain this to me. Nothing like this has ever happened to me before. It was very peculiar. I do hope this isn't a prelude to my going completely mad.

Love,
Windy

10

At two in the morning in New York, I was trying to sleep and fantasizing love-making with Windy. About eight in the morning in London—the very time Windy said she had her experience of me making love to her. A strange coincidence!

11

Perhaps it wasn't a coincidence. The annals of psychical research tell of cases in which a person tries to project himself to visit another and, without being conscious of anything himself, appears to the person. I once knew an icon maker from New York, (originally a farmer from Vermont), who said he once willed himself to appear to a girlfriend in Virginia. Much to the dismay of his friend, his face appeared at her bedroom window.

12

After my experience with Windy, I decided to investigate the phenomenon of *astral sex*. According to occult teachings, each of us has a double, or mental body—an astral, or "starlight" body. The belief in such a body is ancient and worldwide. Plato refers to it in several dialogues. This star body is said to glide from its physical envelope during sleep, and wander off freely in space.

Did some part of me, some phantom projection of my ardent self cut loose from my body, "fly" across the Atlantic ocean, and make love to a distant person?

13

Tall thin Shiela was cheerful and optimistic, though her life was marred by freaky mishaps, abusive co-workers, and auto accidents that turned into complicated legal hassles. But Shiela's main problem was her lover. Oscar was serving time in a penal institution, upstate New York. At first she visited him every week, but that got too expensive. She missed him; it was very frustrating.

Sheila had read a book on astral projection. She decided to give this occult art a try, so she could leave her body and be with the man she loved. She told me exactly what she did: She combined imagery, relaxation, and controlled breathing. The essence of her technique was to mesh her strong impulses with her imagination—the eye of her soul.

It took a while, but at last she managed to launch her astral double on a flight to her lover. Late one evening when she was feeling very lonely, she said, she suddenly found herself with her darling Oscar.

She couldn't confirm the reality of her trip to me in any way; but I was sure she had *some* kind of experience, and wasn't just telling me a tall tale.

After a while, Sheila learned a technique for bringing on the first stages of an out-of-body experience. Unfortunately, she ran into a snag. Relaxing very deeply and visualizing herself leaving her body, she felt herself go deeper and deeper into herself. This was marked by a tingling in her skin, an erotic feeling that occasionally rose to a pitch exciting her to orgasm.

However, if she went too deeply into the experience, she started to feel detached from her body. This frightened her. Her hands and feet became cold and numb, and she felt as if she was going to die. The more pleasurable the sensation, the more sharply she pulled back from the terror of dying. When last we spoke, Sheila had cooled on her jailed lover, but not on her occult studies. With her flair for persistence in the face of obstacles, she learned to navigate the thin line between eros and death anxiety.

Yet, no matter how hard she tried, she couldn't remain long in the first stage of her astral excursion, which was marked by an incomparable erotic sensation. The fear of death prevented her from going all the way. Dawdling at the precipice of a full-blown astral projection produced in her a new species of pleasure. It was a sensation that outclassed anything ordinary sex had to offer; it was certainly better than pining away for her jailed lover. She sent Oscar some books on astral projection, but he never thanked her for them.

14

A man—a soft-spoken black from North Carolina—longed to be with his girlfriend who lived in New York City. Jeff, who had a droll and fatalistic philosophy, was unable to come north and join his girl. He was out of a job, living with his mom.

"It *is*, " Jeff would say. Whenever he met with some hurdle in life, he would pronounce his favorite oracle: "It *is*. "

Jeff, unlike Sheila, wasn't trying to visit his girl in New York. It just happened one night while he was daydreaming. He had been thinking about her, missing her. Suddenly he found himself standing by a doorway in a strange apartment. He looked inside to a dimly lit room. It appeared to be a bedroom with old movie posters on pale green walls. He noticed a dead roach in an ashtray, mixed with cigarette butts. Hovering there in his dream-lucid state, Jeff saw his girlfriend. She was lying naked on the bed, sipping a glass of wine. Then, stepping out of nowhere it seemed, another man appeared. Also entirely naked. The shock of seeing his girl like this ended his experience, and he found himself back in his bedroom, his heart pounding like a jackhammer.

Was it a dream? He insisted it wasn't. The experience was too vivid. Jeff roused himself, gathered up a few belongings, and set out north. Arriving in New York, he went straight to his girlfriend's apartment, and found her living with another man. A shoe salesman!

Jeff stayed in New York, his girl married her new man and returned to North Carolina with him. This experience confirmed Jeff's fatalism. When I asked him how he thought it was possible to leave his body, all he could say was: "It is. You are. I am."

With further questioning, however, I found that despite his outwardly calm manner, Jeff was a jealous man, though he hated to admit it. He was always jealous of his girl, and suspected all along that something was wrong. He spent many an hour wondering what she was up to. He found out.

15

Such stories—as well as my own experiences—seem to show that need and passion may sometimes cause our minds to separate from our bodies. My astral sex experience got me to thinking about the infamous incubi and succubi—male and female spirits said in earlier times to sexually molest the living. Many women during the European witch-craze were tortured and executed on account of their alleged sex relations with demons. They often confessed to having amorous relations with incorporeal entities.

We of course dismiss such claims as ridiculous. Where did the story of the witch's nightflight and sex with demons come from in the first place? I suspect there may have been occasionally been some psychic kernel of truth to these experiences. Not a kernel that supports the witch-hunters, of course. On the other hand, I think there may have been more to these stories than most present day "rationalists" are likely to admit.

16

I wonder what really happens when we surrender to nightly sleep. Most of our erotic dreams no doubt reflect our private hankerings; but perhaps some of them register moods, images, and fantasies afloat in the astral airwaves, bits and pieces of other soul-longings attracted to us by our secret sympathies.

It has yet to be written: the epic of the collective dream brothel of the human mind. What tender flights, forbidden escapades, and rank orgies transpire in the nightside of our soul life!

17

I want to end with a note on sex after death. Many people spurn the idea of an afterlife; the prospect bores them, they say, for without a body, there could be no sex.

This is a parochial complaint, but it is also based on a feeble imagination of the possibilities. From a logical point of view, we don't need a body to have sensuous experiences. For example, our dream life is purely mental.

Nevertheless, as most of us probably know, our dream experiences can be intensely sensuous. The blues I have seen in my dreams were bluer than any sky I ever saw with my physical eyes. The sun I experienced in my dreams was more brilliant than any seen with my waking powers of sight. Yet—and this is the philosophical point—no physical stimuli produced these images; they were pure products of mind.

Now, I have little doubt that most readers of these pages have had erotic dream experiences. And anyway, we all know how important fantasy is in these matters. In the afterlife, love would be all fantasy. The possibilities are breathtaking!

Sex after death would vary, spanning the heights and depths; it would be as gross or as subtle, as selfish or as beautiful, as the souls that we brought with us into the next world.

So let us put the body in perspective; what's important is to care for soul. For without soul, sex in any possible world—on earth or in heaven—is bound to be a thing of small worth.

Believing as I do that man in the distant future will be a far more perfect creature than he now is, it is an intolerable thought that he and all other sentient beings are doomed to complete annihilation after such long-continued slow progress.

Charles Darwin

Chapter Twelve
A Surprise Visit

Sometime in 1974 I awoke one morning and found myself floating above my body. The room was filled with sunlight; everything looked normal. Yet somehow I was standing outside myself! The Greeks had a word for this: *ek-stasis*—ecstasy.

I noticed something odd. In addition to my bedroom, I saw a montage of green hills and blue sky. I had slipped into a kind of dual consciousness. It felt as if I could go anywhere I wished. Then I asked myself: What if I can't make it back? The moment I had this thought, I bounced back into my body, my heart pounding like mad.

Did I really leave my body? Or was it just a trip in the imagination? Come to think of it: Does it make sense at all to talk about a *person* leaving his body?

After all, when Jack is on the corner waiting for Jill, he's waiting to spot a body. A fleshless Jill isn't what Jack expects—or wants. Subtract the body and you seem to subtract Jill. Nothing seems left over to count as the Jill that makes Jack's heart flutter.

Out-of-body flight! The idea is outrageous! The out-of-body experience is a provocative phenomenon. It raises questions about our self-image, our personal identity. It raises questions about our future.

2

Are OBEs, in fact, harbingers of our psychic evolution? Evolution shows an important trend: Life seems progressively to master all environments. Life began in the sea, learned to clamber onto land, then took to the air. The more organized a living creature—the greater the trend to explore and master the natural world. Most remarkable is the form of life called humanity. Through Homo sapiens, life has explored every niche of the terrestrial globe; it has also begun to explore outer space.

Humankind is evolving *into* space; no doubt about that. But is it also evolving *beyond* space? May Mind, the evolutionary apex of life, be struggling to evolve its *own* space?

Well, for one thing, our minds already "occupy" their own spaces. When we dream, for instance, our dream experiences occur in their own space. After all, *where* did last night's dream occur? One's brain may have been on Main Street, USA, but it makes no sense to say that the events of one's dream were occurring on Main Street. When I dream of an old friend, my mind creates its own space to accommodate my meeting with him.

This is remarkable. In dreams our minds create their own spaces. But what of Mind in general? Is Mind as a whole struggling to create a new dimension, a new geography, a new environment? Are we collectively creating a new space—an "inner" space—where, in the imagination of the species, we can pursue our evolutionary adventure? Given the record of cosmic evolution, its history of producing marvels of novelty, it would be unwise to arbitrarily limit the possibilities.

3

Skeptics will of course protest. OBEs are projections of imagination, they will say, vivid fantasies we construct from memory and desire. Psychological tricks for escaping stress. Some OBEs may best be explained this way. But not all.

Certain OBEs aren't *just* imaginary. Such OBEs are called *veridical.* In a veridical OBE, there is more than a subjective sensation of being located out of your body; the experience has earmarks of objective reality. One claims to *verify* being located elsewhere. This type of OBE, if supported by evidence, packs a theoretical punch. There is no obvious way to "scientifically" explain veridical OBEs.

Veridical OBEs say something about life after death. If you can detach your consciousness from your body while you're alive, maybe you can detach it after death. Death might just be a long out-of-body experience.

4

There are two types of veridical OBEs. In one you paranormally acquire some bit of information. In the other you paranormally influence the physical environment. The latter, in my opinion, is the stronger type: The OB traveler moves, knocks about, or otherwise influences some physical object. Cases like this, if genuine, would be tough to dismiss as "mere" imagination. Examples exist in the literature, but they are rare.

Luckily, I myself was involved in an OBE where a physical object was moved. Experiences like this help us picture the possibility that Mind may be evolving beyond physical space.

5

Like many people I've known, Elizabeth was glad to find someone who would listen to her experiences, and not regard her as a nominee for the nearest lunatic asylum. I was glad to listen, not only because the experiences were interesting but also because Liz had a critical mind.

Out-of-body experiences were common in Liz's life, but after hearing her stories, I was uncertain if her OBEs were subjective or objective. "The out-of-body experience has been part of my life since early childhood," she wrote in her diary, adding candidly: "They've always served as an escape mechanism for me—a way to fly away from my mother's cancer and cardiac condition and my father's very visible Parkinson's disease with its accompanying tremors."

Liz says she was a shy child, preferring to read by herself rather than play with other children. Her mother had groomed her for convent life, filling her head with stories of a certain Bayonne nun, a Sister Miriam Teresa, an ecstatic and stigmatist.

"My mother taught me to accept the miraculous."

As a child she liked to sit in the backyard swing and put herself in a trance. Sometimes these trances turned into out-of-body trips.

"I could observe myself," she writes, "from several feet away, sitting quietly on the swing, escaping from the minor chaos, typical in a family with six children." These experiences, usually spontaneous, were frequent in her teens. In time she learned to spot "body cues" that started her out-of-body journeys.

Once she realized her OBEs were a little odd, she became reluctant to discuss them with others. She wondered if they were a foretaste of religious ecstasy. She became a postulant at the Sisters of the Good Shepherd in Peekskill, NY, in the fall of 1967. However, once she started college, she lost her religious vocation, developed an interest in anthropology, married, and had three kids.

6

During her second childbirth, Liz had an OBE. Prepared for natural childbirth, she refused all pain-killers and wanted to keep her glasses on. Without them (her eyesight was 20/200), she would feel "frantic" and "out of control." Hospital policy prevailed; Liz removed her glasses. While giving birth to her daughter, Krissi, she had an experience: "I suddenly felt the familiar sensation of my entire essence being lifted up from the abdominal downward pressure as the baby's head crowned, and I felt myself being literally pulled from a space at the top of my head into the space above me. I was out, and I could observe myself on the delivery table *clearly*. My vision was perfect; I watched the baby emerge from my body without fear or pain."

In her out-of-body state, her vision became normal.

Liz soon became a Registered Nurse, and helped deliver many babies. She wrote of her daughter Krissi's birth. The baby was "delivered textbook perfect. I can still see her head emerge and then turn to permit each shoulder to be delivered. Then the rest of her body slid easily out of me. I felt drawn to her at that instant and found myself once again reconnected to 'myself,' holding the baby on my stomach, as the doctor waited for the blood in the umbilical cord to stop pulsating. Then he cut the cord and we became two separate beings."

When I met Liz in the mid 70s, she was still having OBEs, sometimes several a week. By this time she had developed some degree of control over them and had learned to pilot her nearby environment. For example, she visited her mother, who lived on the other side of town, watched her play solitaire, then phoned to confirm her out-of-body observation. Her OB jaunts had become commonplace.

7

One day I invited Liz to pay me a visit—that is, an out-of-body visit. I made the invitation offhand, as I often do to people who say they can leave their bodies. Not long after—it was autumn—something happened that jarred my sense of what was humanly possible.

8

In 1976 I was living alone on Woodlawn Avenue in Jersey City on the top floor of a two-family house. The apartment had six rooms. The living room was long and narrow with wood-panelled walls. Recently I had taken up the flute. An inspired beginner, methodical in practice, I kept my music-stand in one spot by the window, beside the bookcase. Waking up, I normally went to this spot, assembled my flute and played progressive exercises from Garibaldi or Marcel Moyse.

It had become my morning ritual: standing at the same place, mindful of breath, fingering, embouchure. I liked the room's narrow shape, the trio of windows and the maple-dotted street. Every object in the room had a special home. I mention this to make a point: I kept my stand in one spot.

9

I woke up one morning, and found the music-stand right in the middle of the living-room—completely out of place. How did it get there? I knew *I* didn't move it. No one had been in the apartment but me for days. The old couple who owned the house, and lived below, wouldn't enter my rooms. I had to conclude—though I found it hard to believe—that I unconsciously moved the stand myself.

I put the incident out of mind. Later that afternoon Liz called. Again, in her own words: "I was in my bedroom studying. I felt the familiar sensation of leaving my body. I was alert and very excited that the experience was occurring. I remember vividly the rushing sensation, as the top of my head seemed to open and free me from the body sitting on the bed, book in hand. I wanted to tell Michael. I felt very powerful. It seemed important to contact him. It was like the feeling of anticipation one gets at the prospect of surprising a friend with a visit.

"As Michael's student, I was aware that he lived several blocks from the college. I decided to concentrate on him and felt confident that I could somehow find him. For an instant I found myself outside in the dark, noticing stars, street, familiar houses. Then, in a flash, I was crossing the Hackensack River.

"The next second, I found myself in a kitchen, and saw Michael sitting at a small table by the window, books and papers spread out around him. A few dishes were piled in the sink and some dusty figurines lined the window. The room was bright and seemed very warm. Michael had his back to me.

"My first thought was to tap him on the shoulder and say, 'Hi!—I made it.'

"It felt like the first time I rode a bicycle or danced in perfect step with a man. 'Look at me!' I wanted to say. 'This is important. This is what I told you I would try to do.' I didn't want to frighten

Michael. I moved around until I was next to him and willed him to sense my presence. I touched his hand. He responded by reaching for a cup of tea. As he sipped his tea, and glanced down at his book, I realized that he couldn't see or feel me. I felt frustration and defeat. I was so close to him that I could touch him. I tried to tug on his beard. He leaned backward in his chair and stretched his arms over his head.

"He'll never believe this, I thought. I can't prove to him that I was here. I was extremely annoyed. I decided to look around to find a way to prove my presence. I went through the kitchen into the book-lined living room. Looking back through the rooms into the kitchen, I watched Michael continue to read and write, unaware of my presence. I realized that the music-stand was the best thing in the apartment I could use to persuade him I was there.

"I decided to attempt to move the stand and felt as if I were able to physically reach out and lift it into the center of the room. Suddenly I saw the stand in the center of the room, looking very much out of place. Michael was still sitting in the kitchen, drinking tea and reading. 'Great,' I thought, 'I went through all this trouble, and he doesn't even notice. I hope he falls over it!'

"I decided to end the experiment and return to my body. Seconds later, I was jolted back in my body and found myself sitting on my bed, the open book still in my hand."

10

And so my invisible caller departed, somewhat in a huff. I noticed nothing all night, absorbed in my books and my papers. It was in the morning that I noticed the stand out of place. Later that day, Liz called; she asked if I liked the new furniture arrangement. She then described her OBE in great detail. She said she tried to move the music-stand—to the middle of the room. *Just where I found it!*.

Before she phoned, she described her experience to a mutual acquaintance, Henry Schlotzhouer. She told him about the stand. We all agreed it was an odd way for a lady to visit a friend!

11

I can, of course, produce an explanation to calm professional debunkers. It may have just been a series of remarkable coincidences. I myself may have unwittingly moved the stand. The evening I sat in my kitchen reading, writing, and drinking tea (that part of her account was also true), Liz may have been home, reading in bed.

As we know, a young, fantasy-prone woman, lying alone in bed, might go off in a trance at a moment's notice. Evidently she did that night and hallucinated leaving her body, flying over the Hackensack river, arriving at my house and watching me do just what I happened in fact to be doing. We must further assume she also hallucinated moving just the music-stand I myself had uncharacteristically and unconsciously moved. I leave it to reader to decide if this explanation is plausible.

12

A question: Why was Liz (in her out-of-body state) able to move a music-stand, which, with music sheets, weighed over three pounds—but couldn't pinch my cheek or pull my beard?

The answer may lie in her remark: "I didn't want to frighten Michael."

We're probably afraid of our psychic power. (In my opinion, with good reason.) The present case may be an illustration. It may have upset Liz to think she could intrude on my person.

Let me conclude with two comments on Liz's story: First, she grew up in an environment that encouraged belief in miracles. According to Liz, her three children also have OBEs. Could there be some unknown genetic factor? So far there is no evidence for genetic coding of psi abilities.

Rather, the evidence is that an environment of belief, acceptance, and expectancy increases the probability of OBEs. (For instance, the so-called "sheep-goat" effect in parapsychology states that if you believe in psychic power you are more likely to have a psychic experience.) What counts are psychic factors. Whatever opens us to the "impossible"—hope, faith, imagination—increases the probability of the "impossible."

Need offers a second clue to the mystery of OBEs. Liz's out-of-body experience, by her own admission, served as an "escape mechanism." To the skeptic, the implications are clear: If the motive is escape, the experience must be illusory, a denial of some painful reality, nothing more. This may be true for some OBEs, but not for the one under discussion. "Illusions" don't move music-stands around.

Having a need doesn't necessarily imply neurotic flight from reality. Having a need may create the conditions necessary for new realities. If needs generate evolutionary energies, we should acknowledge our deepest needs. Our need to transcend death might be shaping our future; OBEs may foreshadow an afterlife environment. Now we will look a little more closely at this possibility.

The secret cause of all suffering is mortality itself, which is the prime condition of life. It cannot be denied if life is to be affirmed.
Joseph Campbell

PART SEVEN
DEATH AND THE SOUL

The soulmaker must at last face death, the ultimate obstacle to the human journey. The modern view is that death is the end. There is no such thing as a soul—a self separate from the body—hence there can be no survival of bodily death.

The traditional view sees death not as the end but as a new beginning; the soul leaves the body at death—it is not destroyed. One of Plato's words for death was *appallage* —departure. Death is a voyage. The soul departs from the body and travels about, as it seems to do, temporarily, in the out-of-body experience.

In the next four chapters, I'm going to tell some stories that suggest that our souls do somehow survive bodily death. They provide data for mapping the far side of soulmaking.

Is death the final stumblingblock to soulmaking? The main point of this book is that to answer such questions, we should look to experience, not to "the authorities." Given my own experiences—and I know I'm not alone on this score—I can say there are no grounds for being cocksure about what death is. Death remains an event of high strangeness.

The discovery that there was a life in man independent of blood and brain, would be a cardinal, a dominant fact, in all science and all philosophy.

Frederic W. H. Myers

Chapter Thirteen

Tinkering With Last Things

In the pantheon of reality-shaping ideas, time's majestic brother is death. As with time, so with death, anomalies exist that deserve our attention.

2

For a moment, let us look at death from the viewpoint of life as a whole. From that viewpoint we could say—though it may sound odd—that there really is no death. For in a way death is an abstraction from nature. In nature, life and death are intertwined, the warp and woof of one fabric, one process. In nature, say the Hindu sages, everything is food for everything. All living organisms are forever taking life from one another. In the ecology of the whole, death is the way life renews itself.

Measured against the great scheme of life's collective enterprise, the individual counts for little. What counts is the average, the reproduction of the type. The individual is an aspect of the whole system of life. This system depends on planet Earth, and life is the byproduct of complex ecosystems. No individual, no species is exempt from the laws that govern the system. Life is an eternal round dance with death.

3

But for us there's a complication called consciousness. Thanks to consciousness, we take death personally.

Consciousness is the power to evoke images. We form an image of things as a whole and of ourselves in relation to that whole. One day we wake up and ask: Who are we? What are we? Where did we come from? Where are we going?

If we weren't conscious beings, world-picture-makers, these questions would never trouble us, and we would pass through nature, without fanfare or tragic consequence.

Whether a philosopher or a plain person, you have a picture of your place in the scheme of things. It may be a refined and (you may think) logical picture, or it may be vague and incoherent, a leftover from family upbringing or half-forgotten religious teachings. Worse, it may be a mean picture imposed on you by the harshness of life. You may feel a need to change your life-picture or you may accept it unquestioningly. Either way, it makes a difference in the way you live your life—as well as in the way you die your death. As conscious beings, we are forced to form some kind of "big" picture.

4

Once I see myself as a body, the idea of my death is born. We humans have a specially sharp image of our mortality. As a rule, the more ego-centric we are, the more disquieting the idea of death will be to us. Consciousness of our mortality seems to have been an unfortunate offshoot of evolution. What was the point of nature letting us see that we have to die?

Nature seems to have been unkind. She might have pruned the growth of our consciousness—kept our awareness down to the bare needs of survival. Of course, most people are pretty engrossed in the struggle for survival. The irony is that the moment we can afford being conscious for its own sake, we trouble ourselves with metaphysical puzzles. Consciousness creates as many problems as advantages for survival. Did Mother Nature screw up here?

5

I sometimes think that mysticism is a brilliantly disguised return to the unconscious body of nature, a technique hit upon for handling the pain of being too conscious. Abandon that grasping ego-obsessed self, say these wily masters, submerge yourselves in God, in Nature, in Cosmic Consciousness. Abolish thought and personality and free yourself from being conscious of mortality!

6

What a shock to the mind of life! All individuals, even the most complex and evolved—mortal! Might this shock have set into motion new forces to create a new form of life? *A form of life capable of immortality?*

We usually assume there is or there isn't a life after death. But there is a third possibility. Life after death, like mind itself, may be a product of evolution. As life itself presumably evolved out of dead matter, perhaps a new form of life—free from the constraints of matter—is also evolving. (We touched on this in the last chapter.) All the ambiguous hints of an afterlife—ghosts and reincarnation memories and out-of-body experiences—may in fact be signs of an *emerging* sphere of afterlife.

7

In the course of human evolution, we observe a new fold in the development of life: the appearance of a new layer, dimension, zone of being into which we seem to be dilating. This new zone of being we call Mind, a realm built up and fused together from the total history of individual minds on earth; a realm, I conjecture, that has slowly acquired a will of its own, a life independent of the bodies it originally was linked to. This greater Earth Mind or Mind at Large is still embryonic. We, our thoughts and deeds here on earth, are the seeds of its morphogenesis.

8

But we are moving too fast! In this and the next three chapters, I want to set down some stories that bear on this grand prospect. If I am right about this new fold in the evolution of Mind, we shouldn't be surprised to meet with facts that suggest survival beyond the grave.

Let me first remind you that quite a bit of data exists on this subject. Psychical researchers have gathered all kinds of information suggestive of an afterlife. Eminent Victorians like Frederic Myers, Henry Sidgwick, Eleanor Sidgwick, and William Barrett, to name just four prominent scholars of the period, left detailed reports of hauntings, apparitions of the dead, and mediumistic phenomena. Much of it gives reason to suspect that in some as yet unclear way we do survive death.

As time went on, the English scholars sought better evidence. Unfortunately, this rich fund of material lies nearly forgotten in the dusty archives of the British and American Societies for Psychical Research.

Not that people have lost interest in life after death. But what is currently taken as proof of survival is inferior to the evidence available. For example, stories of the near-death experience (whose significance lie elsewhere than in "proof" for life after death). Ditto for most talk of "past lives," which is more therapy than evidence for an afterlife.

Not only is the evidence better than most skeptics or believers realize but the objections to it are also more subtle. Let me explain.

9

Early people believed in life after death. What convinced the first people that we survive death?

One possibility was the realism of dreams. In dreams the dead appear to return to us. Early people failed to realize in what sense dreams, for all their impressive realism, were phantasms of their own minds. The modern and more subtle objection to survival is based on a similar type of supposed misinterpretation of psychic fact.

Consider the following. Suppose, in a waking state, I see the apparition of a deceased person. And suppose this apparition reveals information that I couldn't have gotten by normal means: for example, that such and such a person died in an auto wreck, was wearing a baseball cap, and listening to Bach's third flute sonata on his tape deck.

Would an apparition revealing this knowledge prove survival? Perhaps not, says the sophisticated skeptic. I may have used my own psychic powers to learn the facts and then produced a phantasm of the deceased person. What looks like evidence for life after death is really evidence for a fantastic ability of the living to engage in unconscious self-deception.

(This genius for self-deception, if it be fact, should make us all wonder about the beliefs we cherish so confidently.)

Researchers are aware of the ambiguity of survival evidence. Some say that the psychic powers of living people don't account for the best cases. Great mediums like Leonora Piper (studied by William James) or Gladys Osborne Leonard (studied by Sir Oliver Lodge) often reproduced exact bodily gestures, peculiar intonations, and distinctive speech patterns of particular deceased persons. They sometimes obtained copious amounts of accurate information from their disembodied contactees, information not available to the medium by normal means.

Were these mediums such incredibly good self-deceivers? Or do the dead survive, after all?

The phenomena of "cross-correspondence" are often cited as strongly suggestive of survival. This twist in survival research occurred after Myers' death. It appears that *after* death, Myers and other (deceased) researchers devised an experiment to show they had survived death and still had their wits about them in the "next" world. (This is important; we don't want to survive as sub-persons or cretins.)

The ingenious Victorians, apparently from a realm beyond the grave, began to transmit separate bits of information to different mediums around the world. There was Kipling's sister in India, James' master medium, Leonora Piper, in Boston, and the actress-medium, Mrs. Leonard, in London. These bits of information, scattered among the various mediums, included very scholarly references to Greek and Roman antiquities. By themselves they made no sense, either to the individual mediums or to the sitters who were present.

In time, like pieces of a jigsaw puzzle, the scattered messages were joined together and a meaningful picture revealed. The effect seemed to imply the existence of an intelligence, independent of the mediums, working from the "other side." There is quite a bit of this material. The "experiment" went on for years. For any Sherlock Holmes of the psychic realm, many unsolved mysteries remain.

10

My aim here is not to report or weigh this evidence. I just want to assure the reader that it exists and forms the background of these chapters.

My experiences are at odds with the picture of reality I obtained from my education. In recollecting them, I'm trying to recollect myself and thus remake my soul by remaking my world-picture.

The scientific world is loaded with experts. But there are no experts on Last Things—on what is called eschatology. Here we have to rely on our own tinkering.

In the search for answers, there are two sources: history and our own lived experiences. Truth hides in the interplay between the narrow certainties of subjectivity and the broad generalities of history. In this book, I'm trying to burrow my way into soul-nourishing truth from the gut end of my own experiences.

11

People sometimes ask if I believe in ghosts. Of course I do, I always say. That is, I believe that people *experience* certain elusive and mysterious things called ghosts, spirits, wraiths, fetches— things that go bump in the night. It's not a question of belief; I know such experiences are real. They are as common today as they were in ancient Greece or Sumeria. The controversy lies in how to interpret them.

12

A ghost with halitosis may sound like a joke, but my experience was no laughing matter. Once again the scene was the house on Woodlawn Avenue—in haunted Jersey City. I lived in this old wooden house during the early nineteen seventies. It was the house where my friend Liz paid me a visit in her "astral" body.

One winter's night in 1975, I went to sleep after midnight. It had been an uneventful day; nothing unusual or upsetting had happened. I was sound asleep, alone in my bed, when I was awakened about four in the morning by something getting into bed with me.

The bed was a twin. I was sleeping on the right side, facing the window. A slice of crescent moon glowed through a tree branch. Wide awake, I remained still, staring unseeingly at the moon. In my head I screamed: *There's something in bed with me!* And it smelled. Fetid, musky, animal-like. I felt its bulky presence beside me. I knew if I turned round, I'd be staring at the damn thing face to face!

I knew what it felt like—somebody getting into bed with me. And this was somebody *or something* that was very heavy. I sank toward the weight. I heard a deep grouse, a gasping sigh that sounded like something coming from a huge cavernous chest. It was breathing heavily! The breath was foul. I lay there, stiffly in place, not daring to move.

After a few long seconds, the bed *slowly* sprang back into shape, and the smell went away.

I reached over, flicked on the lamp, and turned around. Nothing.

13

Was it a dream? For one thing, the powerful odor was unusual. Most dreams are visual, auditory, rarely tactile, rarely olfactory. Was it a case of false awakening?—of seeming to myself to wake up in the dream? Not at all. I didn't wake up a second time. Whatever *it* was—was *why* I woke up in the first place.

And yet it may have been a peculiar sort of dream. A nightmare perhaps, but one that spilled across some boundary into waking reality. A borderland entity.

> *We must none the less admit that invisible beings, far-wandering influences, shapes that may have floated from a hermit of the wilderness, brood over council-chambers and studies and battlefields.*
>
> William Butler Yeats
> Magic

Chapter Fourteen

Ghosts: The Holy and the Unholy

Investigating a haunted house can be a frustrating experience. Ghosts are never as obliging as ghost hunters would like them to be. One sets out on the job in a quixotic spirit. At best one hopes to catch a shadow on the move or detect the odd cold spot. One hardly expects to be attacked by a ghost! But just that happened to me some years ago in a house in North Arlington, New Jersey.

2

The haunting had begun in 1971, long before I came on the scene. Soon after moving in, Sara and Jim Stone began to sense strange presences in the old colonial house: shadowy forms, cold clammy drafts, thumping noises. They heard footsteps, cabinet draws shaking, doors slamming. The focus was at the stairway leading from the kitchen upstairs. The entity liked to appear in the narrow foyer by the bathroom.

Sara had three children. When I first met them in 1975, Steve was two, Sharon three, Carol five. Sharon and Carol have grown up into charming young ladies. Sara is an attractive women, a redhead with a fair complexion.

The females have been the main victims of the ghostly molestations. It didn't take long to see that here was a ghost who was, in Carol's words, a "dirty old man."

What usually appeared was the phantom of a large man, wearing a staid business suit, and a dark fedora that left his face in shadow. When they did see his face, it looked old, grim, but otherwise undistinguished. The phantom was more or less solid; it sometimes appeared headless.

Jim was high strung, an engineer by profession, tough and practical-minded. We discussed his ghostly lodger several times. Once, when he was alone in the house, he noticed a flickering light appear by the stairway, vanish and reappear by the door, then slowly melt away. He opened the door, rushed out and watched a glowing form shamble down the driveway, where it disappeared. Jim, a doubting-Thomas, admits that some elusive but apparently conscious and wilful entity inhabits his house. He never questions the claims of his wife or daughters.

Sara was the most sensitive to the appearances. By and large, they harassed more than terrified her. Some say that spirit appari-tions are vacuous shells of deceased personalities—like dislocated stills that glare at us, mindlessly, across the film of time. When I tried to explain her experience in these terms, Sara laughed.

Her impression was definite: she was being watched by a conscious being—watched, moreover, with lustful curiosity. And the girls agreed that the thing in their house was an *active* intruder.

It often burst in on them while they were bathing or lying about half-naked. One evening, Sara recalls, she was lying in her tub, sipping a glass of cognac, trying to relax from the day's hassles.

Something moved by the doorway. The bathroom was warm and steamy, but she felt a chill. She looked up and saw the figure of a large man.

Sara looked at the figure. She couldn't make out the face, but the rest of the form was distinct. It was watching her. A familiar feeling—of being objectified by sex-hungry eyes.

"Piss off!" she said, and it faded away.

At first she backed off from the apparition, crossing her arms over her breasts; later she threw things—soap bars, shampoo containers—at the intruder. Sara was high-spirited, well read, a woman of strong opinions. At first scared by her uncanny voyeur, she learned to defy him.

One evening she was by herself, again in the tub. The doorknob twisted and shook. She had locked the bathroom door, so she yelled out, thinking it was one of her kids or her husband.

Something shoulderlike heaved itself against the door. The door shook violently. The shaking subsided and started up again. She listened and thought. It seemed more like a show—a sound of violence—that signified nothing. The moment she thought of the ghost's impotence, the ruckus fizzled out, and it was gone.

3

Hauntings, like poltergeists, normally pass with time. It is as if the energy, whatever its source, dissipates. Poltergeists—those noisy paranormal outbreaks linked to adolescents—usually wind down within months. Hauntings can last for years. Seven, at most, say some experts.

Sara's ghost evidently has staying power, for one of its most terrifying visitations took place on January 13, 1986—long after seven years. It was after her mother's death; a new cycle of disturbances had begun.

Early in the morning, Sara was alone in her house. She opened her eyes at the sound of a cawing crow, climbed out of bed, and was about to step into the bathroom. There was a surprise waiting for her in the foyer.

A tall figure—face faintly visible, fedora turned down, greenish dark coat buttoned up tight at the neck—stood before her. He was blocking the door to the bathroom.

The way he was positioned, brazenly cocky, seemed to say, "You won't dare pass me!"

The form commanded the narrow foyer, crowding, riveting her to the spot where she stood. Sara felt vulnerable; her mother's recent death had depressed her so much, she had to be hospitalized for a while. There was talk of electroshock and they had dosed her with lithium. The drugs she took had weakened her. Her usual defense against the ghostly irritant had broken down; the horror impinged on her like salt on an open wound.

She stood there, choked with fear, and stared at the apparition. The ghost reminded her of a man she once knew. He had muscled his way into her bedroom late one night. Sara's fear turned into anger.

She took a step, and the shadowy figure quavered, seeming to swell in the narrow passage. She hesitated, then boldly walked *through* it, clutching the bathroom doorknob. As she passed, she felt a chill on her neck, and smelled something foul. Her heart pounded, her adrenals throbbed.

She slammed the door shut; something banged on the door. Sara cut loose with unladylike curses, then listened carefully: The noise subsided. She sighed with relief, and reached for her toothbrush.

4

Sara was depressed when the ghost appeared. She was having marital problems and one of her daughters was suffering from a possibly life-threatening illness. So maybe we can explain these ghostly peeping-tom incidents. Maybe Sara conjured the whole thing up from her imagination. Maybe her unhappy unconscious created a creature to tease and distract her. Maybe she needed something to distract her from her mundane chores, something to transport her to a strange forbidden world.

Her ghostly apparitions, the skeptic might say, were caused by marital frustration combined with fertile powers of auto-suggestion. Sara's ghost might just be a fantastic artifact of a long lonely night.

But this view has problems. Others—baby-sitters, husband, aunts, friends, children, children's friends, household pets, and finally, myself—experienced her fantasy. This "fantasy" did some peculiar things. The curtain in the cellar window was turned inside out, for example. Someone—or something—had to remove the curtain from the rod and place it back in reverse. The children couldn't have done it; the window was beyond their reach.

All three kids had strange tales to tell. The two year old boy said he saw a wooden crucifix fly around. He spoke of "the guy in the diaper" jumping off the wall. Sara found the crucifix off its hook. The hook was too high for the children to reach. Fastened firmly to the wall—it was impossible for the crucifix to fall by accident.

The two girls, then three and five, told me how they watched paper in the toilet whirl about as if thrown by invisible hands. As they got older, the pretty teenagers complained of the ghost's furtive oglings.

Nor was it a ghost with much respect for religion. When the crucifix was displaced from the wall, I had the idea that a photograph of Padre Pio, put on display, might dampen the entity's thievish spirits. So on two occasions I gave Sara a small photo of the Padre; each time she placed them inside a locked china cabinet. Each time they disappeared.

Other things disappeared: according to Sharon, a small statue of the Virgin Mary. (This was in 1986.) This confirmed the impression that the ghost was impious. It further confirmed that he was a *dirty* old ghost, who scorned the idea of virginity. Not only did the statue of the virgin vanish. Sharon's T-shirts, her jeans, and most often, her underwear, vanished. The kinky overtones of this were obvious.

(How odd to think that if we survive bodily death, some of us may do so as peeping-toms who steal underwear from teenage girls!)

5

After listening to these stories—especially the one about Padre Pio's photos vanishing—I agreed to spend the night in the house.

It was fall in 1975, and after dinner I listened to the children and Jim tell their ghostly tales. Sara took me on a tour of the house.

I stood by the stairway—the spot where the ghost was said to appear. Nothing strange, no mysterious lights, no phantom chills. I was shown the curtains in the basement, turned inside out, their edges unaccountably charred. I examined the washing-machine said to go on by itself, the wall hook the crucifix "jumped off," and so on.

One last nightcap, and it was time to retire. The living room sofa was arranged for me. Sharon brought a pillow and a blanket. We all said goodnight; the dog and two cats withdrew. Propped on the sofa, I leaned back. The embers of a big fire crackled, slowly dying. I scanned the ceiling rafters, glanced at the stairway.

A small lamp glowed in the corner of the room. The curtains were half drawn, and a big elm tree was visible across the street. I was prepared to stay awake. If anything was going to happen, I wanted to be wide awake. Bit by bit, I slumped into the sofa.

I looked at my watch; it was after two.

Then, without warning, I heard, clearly and distinctly, a gong ring. A low soft echo persisted for a fraction of a second.

I stood up and looked around the living room.

High on the wall to the far right—opposite the stairway—hung a large brass Chinese gong. About three feet in diameter, it looked very heavy; a velvet-knobbed stick was attached to it.

"Michael?" Sara in her nightgown, halfway down the stairs, was peering at me through the shadows.

"Did you hear it, too?"

"Somebody struck the gong," she said, eyeing me.

"Well, it sure as hell wasn't me!"

I removed the stick and gently struck the gong. A soft metallic ring—what I heard a moment ago—echoed briefly. Who rang the damn thing? No living person could have. I *knew,* because I was the only one in the room.

So the ghost had announced itself!

Sara went back upstairs and I resumed my watch. A certain climax of tension seemed to have passed. The entity had indeed been obliging, letting me know it was in the house. I heard the gong ring, and so did Sara. So that was that. I thought I might go to sleep now, but the gong kept echoing in my head, and kept me alert. Tossing and turning on the sofa, after a while I calmed down, nestling myself under the blanket. My head at a forty-five degree angle, I was still facing the stairway.

6

I no longer expected anything to happen. It was almost three o'clock in the morning, and I was set for sleep. The moment I said to myself it was time to sleep, I became aware of something in front of me. By the stairway—a form, a faint shimmering oval of pale bluish light. Startled, I raised my head. I saw it with my own eyes: a distinct torso, the vague outline of a head.

I lay on my back, too surprised to feel any emotion. It was just standing there, hovering, a gloomy radiance in suspense. It fluttered, as if from a breeze blowing through the room. I was going to call out when suddenly it moved swiftly forward—*and engulfed me!*

It wrapped itself around me, locking me in the folds of what felt like an iron grip. I tried to raise my right elbow and to shout: "It's here!" But my vocal chords froze. I was paralyzed, locked in a voiceless etheric bubble.

For several seconds, I remained in its grip. I tried to cry out, but couldn't. *It* was curled round me. I could see its hazy outline *face to face!* It was squeezing the life out of me!

Suddenly, it loosened its grip, and was gone. It was gone as quickly as it appeared.

Too late to wake Sara, I lay there, shaken but thrilled with a sense of triumph. Whatever the nature of this entity, it could now claim me as another witness to its existence.

7

The house was haunted. So much I could say with confidence. Haunted by something. But by what? Was it something with a human mind? Had it once lived on earth, walked and talked and loved—a human being? Or was it something more exotic—a demon, an elemental, an alien from ultra space?

I asked Sara to research the history of the house, but we found no evidence of anyone resembling the ghost ever having lived in the house. I concluded that an unknown entity occupied the house.

8

The thing in the North Arlington house smelled evil. So did the thing with halitosis I described in the last chapter. And both were pretty aggressive. Could they have been the same thing?

The ghost may have taken umbrage with me for joining forces with Sara.

"Kick the old bugger out!" I recommended.

My advice was to get tough, act as if she were addressing a conscious, maybe a rational being. As often as possible, I tried to get her to take an active stand against the intruder. In short, educate him. Sara was a confirmed feminist. She had every right to resent being a plaything of masculine whim, most of all the whims of a dead man, a miserable hanger-on between worlds.

To this day I'm not sure if my unbidden bedfellow was the ghost of North Arlington. If they were one and the same, it would be interesting. For if a psychic entity from North Arlington can get angry, follow me to my apartment in Jersey City, and try to scare the daylights out of me, it would have the earmarks of a conscious personality.

9

One point everyone agreed on. The ghostly manifestations and the family's emotional disturbances were linked. When Sara and Jim fought, the kids got sick, or someone died, weird happenings increased. The ghost seemed to thrive on unwholesome emotions. It was, in short, *an unholy ghost.*

The following is an example. September, 1986. A seventeen year old friend of the family, Larry was a talented musician— bright, charming, good-looking. But he had problems with his parents. His father was a cop who nagged him, specially about school; he'd complain if his son got an "A." "Why not A+?" One night the teenager borrowed his dad's gun and shot himself to death.

Soon after the suicide, the apparitions increased around the girls. Carol was the main victim. On the phone with a friend, the heaving against her bedroom door began. The doorknob wriggled from an unseen force; she screamed; the door shook. Her friend, Janet, at the other end of the line, heard the noise. Janet described the whole thing to me.

After Larry's suicide, phenomena increased. The death of Sara's mother also caused phenomena to increase. So did the marital battles, which were more frequent lately, and more intense. It was clear. The more powerful the negative emotions, the more the unholy ghost seemed to thrive.

10

What are we to make of this tie?

Perhaps the apparitions are somehow a reflection of the family's unhappiness. We would have to suppose, if we looked at it this way, that an entity—a group phantasm or hallucination —was built up over the years and acquired a certain quasi-material existence. Moreover, it can turn against its unconscious creators and even influence outsiders like myself. In Tibet such an entity is known as a *tulpa*.

If such entities exist, they are beyond present science. Normal science knows nothing of collective nightmares that pop into physical space, move curtains around, cause photos to vanish, knock crucifixes off the wall, make brass gongs ring, or attack and paralyze a man.

11

Another perspective is this. The emotional fluctuations in the Stone family may allow something *already present in the house to manifest*. Perhaps a disembodied person or a fragment of a psychic system, human or nonhuman, that exists in some unknown manner.

Remember the spirits in Homer's *Odyssey*. They were temporarily revived by sacrifice. Odysseus digs a trench, sacrifices sheep, fills the trench with blood. Odysseus has come for advice from his old fighting companion, Achilles. But sacrificial blood must be poured on the earth. This, says Homer, allows the "specters of those who had died, (to come) up out of Erebos." They become visible, and Achilles talks with Odysseus.

Similarly, the "specter" trapped in the North Arlington house may come to life, charged by the emotional "blood" shed by the Stone family. On this theory, Sara's ghost would be a kind of vampire, a psychic parasite.

12

In any case, death remains a mystery. Too many facts clash with the dogma of sheer extinction. With these odd facts it is possible, I believe, to begin to revise the image of death most of us have acquired from our modern "higher" education.

For instance, we have the idea of unwholesome or unholy ghosts. An unholy ghost thrives on decay and misery, feeding off unwholesome emotions. It would draw its strength, as we said, from the pains of tragic loss and the dregs of broken loves. Out of dark, bitter, disjointed passions a larger, if stranger, life grows, a life with a will of its own, a kind of psychic monster.

13

Let's go a step further. If *unholy* ghosts exist, perhaps there are *holy* ghosts. Perhaps much larger groups of people—not for fifteen but for hundreds, even thousands, of years—cultivate strange haunting relationships.

Just as the entity in North Arlington attracts to itself unwholesome emotions, feeding upon them, and so sustaining itself, so might higher entities attract to themselves the higher hopes, prayers, and aspirations of the living.

For all we know we are haunted by blithe spirits as well as by troubled ghosts. Religions, I've sometimes thought, have something in them akin to great hauntings. Perhaps the great souls who lived on earth—saints and saviors, artists and dreamers—need to haunt us. They may keep us in their hearts and memories after death. It may be one way—it may be the only way—to preserve themselves from drifting into aimlessness or extinction. Religions, at least in their psychically vital aspect, may be hauntings of great souls who need us as much as we need them.

14

For example, Christianity may be one of the great hauntings in human history. According to church doctrine, God has three aspects: The Father and the Son and the Holy Ghost. Since the death of Jesus, the lived psychic reality of Christianity is linked to the experience of the Holy Ghost. This was true for the primitive church. In *Acts of the Apostles,* which records the early history of the Great Christian Haunting, the most compelling figure is a Holy Ghost! The plain fact is this: it isn't the Jesus of flesh and blood who dominates history. What remains, what continues to enchant the world is his psychic image—his elusive Healing Spirit.

15

Holy and unholy ghost differ, as the effect on the sense of smell illustrates. In contrast to the odor of sanctity, a feature of saintly lore, we have in the Stone ghost the odor of deviltry. The odor of sanctity, in fact, is widely reported: Saintly beings are known to produce mysterious fragrances. Even more startling, but also well documented, are reports of the incorrupt corpses of saints and yogis exuding such fragrances.

One wonders about such odors, foul or fragrant. They seem to be rather a product of some supernatural horticulture. This raises an interesting question about afterworld geography. Perhaps when we enter the mindscapes of afterdeath, it will be the quality of our thoughts that shapes the form and substance of our reality.

Perhaps in afterlife worlds, a thought of love becomes a whiff of budding roses, a twinge of sadness turns into a damp wind. The foul smell of the unholy ghost would reveal his thwarted passion, while souls of the holy might leave a fragrance on the great breeze of becoming. All perception would be symbolic, all objects artworks, all worlds expressions of our innermost selves.

*If a man could pass through Paradise in a
dream, and have a flower presented to him as
a pledge that his soul had really been there,
and if he found that flower in his hand when
he awoke—Aye! and what then?*

Samuel Taylor Coleridge

Chapter Fifteen
Dreamchild

By 1974 I had begun to study psychical research. My reputa-
tion as the philosophy professor interested in the "occult" caused
odd reactions. One anxious pedant told students that their lives
would be ruined if they took my courses. Others behaved as if
discussing psychic phenomena might endanger a student's mental
health.

The students themselves had a different view; many of them had
puzzling experiences they needed to discuss with somebody. They
often stayed after class, trailing after me with a look of: "There's
something I must tell you."

I was learning from experience that the world was a much
stranger place than I had reckoned, so it was easy for me to suspend
disbelief, and listen to their experiences, however queer or outland-
ish. In the end, things balanced out: what I lost in respect from
colleagues, I gained in trust from students.

2

Deirdre was such a student, and her story was *very* strange.

She had large green eyes and auburn hair that fell awkwardly
across her face. I sensed her poor posture and shy manners were
ways of shielding you from the full force of her personality—of
which even she was a little afraid.

Her friends and family were bewildered by what occurred
around her. Their way of dealing with her was to deny there was
anything out of the ordinary. Her doctors were excellent deniers.
Her priest denied her with his blessings. Her boyfriend began by
affirming but ended by denying her. Everyone had a theory to
explain, domesticate and normalize Deirdre.

3

She was nineteen when we first met. Her boyfriend, Stan, also a student of mine, (better at poker than philosophy), walked into my office one day and told me a story about "somebody he knew."

This somebody had a remarkable dream about a small boy. The boy—about three years old—wore a white cape. He appeared—in this person's dream—on a shore by a stormy sea.

The boy, threatened by the storm, waved for the girl to help him. Off to the side, huddled together, are the girl's friends and family. They look afraid and cry out: "Don't touch that child!" The girl looks at the child, feels sorry for him, and decides to help. She lifts him up, pressing him to her breasts; the people scream, and the dream ends.

A striking dream, but the sequel is incredible.

According to Stan, when the dreamer awoke and opened her eyes, her right hand was covered with a black sticky substance. She had no idea where it came from. Could she have been walking in her sleep?

It must have come from the dream, she thought.

This idea, as it sank in, disoriented her. But it was true; it looked to her as if the black substance had oozed over the borderline of her dream into waking reality—*an apport from a dream.*

"This really happened," Stan insisted, his normally drowsy face fully animated. "I saw her hand. It was totally black. She didn't walk in her sleep. There wasn't any black paint in the house, either."

Stan gaped at me; I nodded.

"I watched her mother scrub for half an hour. It was damn hard to clean off."

4

Of course, the "somebody" Stan knew was his girl, Deirdre. Before long I gained Deirdre's confidence, and she told me the story herself. I asked her to write it all down and keep a diary of her unusual experiences. Eventually she gave me the diary, which I still have.

The confidence lasted a year. I took notes on our daily meetings and our many lengthy phone calls. Since I was the only person she knew who wouldn't make fun of her, she shared her experiences with me: her dreams, the queer events that dogged her life, even her love-affairs.

5

I see a white seagull fly by; it leaves a trace in my mind in the form of a memory. Might it be possible to reverse this? Why not the image of a seagull in my mind produce a physical counterpart? It would be called materialization—the reverse of memory. If memory is possible, I thought, why not materialization?

Deirdre's dreamchild played havoc with my picture of mind and matter. I remembered Coleridge's odd musing in his notebooks: "If a man could pass through Paradise in a dream, and have a flower presented to him as a pledge that his soul had really been there, and if he found that flower in his hand when he awoke—Aye! and what then?"

A dream, a piece of which, oozes over into waking reality? An unsettling but a marvelous thought! A careful collector of pictures of hyper-reality, this one taxed my boggle-threshold. To bring something back from a dream? Even if it were only a flake of dried mud, what a dizzying expansion in our view of what is possible! It was of course impossible. Still, I had seen so many "impossible" things myself, I tried to listen to Deirdre's story without making her feel as if she were crazy.

She dreamt the dream more than once, and whenever she touched the child in her dream, she awoke with her hand covered by a mysterious black substance. There was no question that she, her boyfriend, and her mother thought this was true. Her mother, a superstitious woman, forced her to clean her hand at once. To prevent the whole thing from happening, Deirdre, who apparently could control her dreams, refused to touch the child when he begged her help. As it turned out, it was a request she wasn't meant to refuse.

6

I wanted proof of Deirdre's psychic powers, and decided to perform a little experiment. She and Stan were enrolled in my course on Eastern metaphysics. Classwork included practical exercises in meditation.

I asked students to close their eyes, and meditate on a visual target I was looking at (concealed from their view, of course). The aim of the experiment was to dream the target that night. They were to leave a written report in my office the following morning. Since I selected and concealed the target, no one but myself knew its contents.

The results were startling. No one came close to a hit—except Deirdre. The target was an illustration from page 362, Volume Six, of *Man, Myth, and Magic.* It portrays a group of penitents in black robes following an effigy of the Crucified Christ through the streets of Seville. According to her written account, Deirdre dreamt of "a bright vivid sky with clouds. . .two black cylindric shapes that reminded me of towers. . .you observed them from a slant. . .on the right hand side a very large tree. . .the area in which I was standing seemed to be some sort of cobblestone section. . .I received the impression there was some type of altar. . .was peaceful and anxious, serene yet as if something exciting were going to happen."

All she wrote was on mark. The reader can refer to the original photo. She had the tree on the correct side. The black, slanting cylindrical forms—two main ones in the foreground—nicely evoked the hooded penitents. The sky was indeed bright blue with some clouds, and indeed in the foreground, the road was covered with cobblestones. The effigy in the photograph was mounted on an altar. Even the words she used to describe the scene's mood fit: Good Friday, the occasion for the outdoor ceremony, might well be described as peaceful and anxious, serene and pregnant with excitement. Either her performance was a wild co-incidence or Deirdre had exceptional dream skills.

7

About a month after this series of dreams began, Deirdre dreamt she was in an auto accident. Another girl was driving, she added. I asked her to write it down.

A week later, she walked into my classroom with her right arm in a sling. She had been in an auto accident that morning. Driving to work, her *girlfriend* ran a red light, and the car crashed into a mail truck. Deirdre's right hand went through the windshield.

It was frustrating; she had just taken up painting. An impulse had come to her out of nowhere—to study art. At first she had a vague impulse to put certain colors, the moods they evoked, into visual images. She'd pass by an art supplies shop, and feel like buying a paint set. She had never taken an art class.

One night she dreamt of the child: he asked her to paint *him*. In fact, her first experiments in painting and her dreamchild encounters began at the same time. She found herself trying to paint her dream: the child in peril at the seashore, the white cape, the strange angelic eyes, the storm and the mysterious black substance. Her accident occurred right after she started painting.

The injured hand became discolored—and *turned black*. The hand didn't heal. This was only the beginning. A fantastic web of events unravelled from the moment Deirdre chose to rescue her dreamchild.

First, the car crash in which her hand—*as in her dream*—turned black. Then a train of accidents, illnesses, and offbeat incidents; every day she called there was something.

Here are some entries from her diary.

October 15, 1974.
"I went to the store this afternoon for groceries. My neighbor has a Doberman. Known him for years—a friendly dog. He turned on me, nasty bite, drawing blood. Sleeve from a new blouse, torn to shreds.

*October 17. "A strange man appeared in the neighborhood this afternoon. Filthy, dressed in a black suit. He had funny oriental eyes. He stared at me, and then he began to follow me. When I turned and looked at him, he called me names. He shouted curses. The man was demented."

*October 18."A visit from an old boyfriend. Out of the blue, he's standing on my doorstep, knocking madly on my door. What do you want? I ask him. He starts to blame me for his life, he has it in for me, he's going to get me. I force the door shut, Jacko goes on knocking, screaming he's going to kill me.

*October 21. "I came into work today. A large metal cabinet, very large and very heavy, just toppled over as I walked by it. Hawkmyer flew into a rage. Fired."

*October 22. "Stan was trying to teach me how to drive today. On the empty part of the Turnpike, just before Exit 16. The car went on fire. Got to a service station. Mechanics couldn't figure out why it happened. Stan is furious. He blames me!"

*October 25. "I was sitting by the window. There was a thunderstorm. Lightning struck the metal rod in the sling on my right arm. The sling split in two and flew off my arm. Is there a message here?"

8

There was a pattern to the events, and the key to it was her painting. The moment she quit painting her dreamchild, everything seemed to join ranks in a conspiracy against her. Even the random forces of nature turned against her—like the lightning that struck her sling. An old boyfriend suddenly began to remember (or conjure up) bad feelings toward her. For no apparent reason, stray men, even dogs in the street, unloaded their hostility on her. Even an inanimate metal cabinet— poltergeist-like—seemed to acquire a will of its own and set out to punish her. Animism with a vengeance!

Somehow the dreamchild was behind all this. At first she dreamt of him every night. Sometimes he would appear above her when she drowsed. He became her interior guide—a mouthpiece of esoteric wisdom. In exchange for rescuing him from the storm, he counseled her on psychic and spiritual matters. She repeated the discussions she had with him, and I was surprised by the depth of the thought.

Her dreamchild gave her practical instructions—mostly in opposition to her mother and boyfriend. The "child" wanted her to paint a picture of him, for instance; he urged her to become an artist. The accident occurred after quarrelling with her mother about becoming an artist.

"Little Miss Michelangelo," her mother would say, who felt a degree in accounting was the better path to a happy life.

9

When Deirdre ignored her dreamchild, things went badly for her. When she followed his instructions, her hand started to heal, the mishaps stopped, and her life took a turn for the better. That was the pattern. The tough thing was that everyone was against taking the child in the white cape seriously.

I took him seriously, and the reason why was simple: when Deirdre acted in harmony with her dreamchild, she got better. It made perfect sense: deny the dreamchild in ourselves and most of us are likely to suffer. Deny the creative needs of the soul and the soul sickens.

10

People around Deirdre had three views of her dreamchild. Her mother and friends had a superstitious fear of all things psychic. Her doctors—and her priest—regarded every psychic tale as an illusion, a misunderstanding, or possibly demon-inspired. Her boyfriend and some of her stranger relatives wanted to *use* Deirdre's magical child. Stan, for instance, liked to drag his psychic girlfriend to poker games, as if she were a live rabbit's foot.

11

I observed many strange things that year of friendship with Deirdre, who seemed like someone who had stepped out of a book of Celtic fairy tales. Let me describe one apparently paranormal dream I had—a dream about as horrifying as any I can recall.

I'm in a room full of old hags, dressed in black. They're standing around a dark mahogany table, which is shaped like a coffin. Atmosphere, lurid, hazy. The women, quarreling, shrieking at each other, like crones in a preternatural rage. I seem to be lying down, as if I were in bed; one of the hags walks up to me and points a gnarled finger at my head.

In a fury she shrieks: "You! You! You!"

The finger, half eaten by the worms of hell, wriggles in my face.

"Deirdre" she screeches, "is in league with Satan!"

The voice I heard was *not* sweet. The effect was so terrifying—the tone so unwholesome—that I started to *faint in the dream.* (I had never fainted in a dream.) Backwards I sank. As I turned to the left, my heart hammering, another horrid old hag, skinny as a skeleton, wearing a tight black gown, rapidly approached me on spidery legs.

The sight of her face so close to mine woke me with a jolt. I opened my eyes. For a split second I felt dizzy. *She was still there!* Standing over me, just as she was in my dream, pointing her hellish finger at my head. "And *you,*" she said, "are in league with Satan!"

I shook myself. The hag vanished.

I lay in the dark for a while, gathering my wits, scanning the shadows. My first thought was, Heck No! I had to nip this horror in the bud. After a few moments, I pulled myself together. My hand was trembling, but I scribbled some notes.

12

It was unlike any dream I ever had. In fact, I hesitate to call it a dream. It was more like a visit to one of the back rooms of hell. Worse than the noisome animal smell of the phantom that once climbed into bed with me, this was darker, thicker, more oppressive. Imagine a place filled with an eternal din of people scolding each other with pious hatred. A postgraduate seminar in the classics, I learned the true meaning of such words as Fury and Horror. I'd seen, or should say, felt pure Evil; it was sticky, carnal, as the ancients understood evil, an obscene stain, a pollution that sickens the soul.

13

Next morning, I reported my experience to Deirdre. She told me a story that shed light on my encounter.

Deirdre had an aunt who died a few years ago. This aunt—her name was Dorothy—lived a life of bitterness and regret. Full of lofty spiritual aspirations, she wanted to enter a nunnery.

But her aspirations were met with derision. Her father made fun of her spiritual fantasies as well as squelched her natural self. For a while Dorothy hoped for a happy marriage, and had a few abortive tries at love.

Dorothy resigned herself to spinsterhood. She blamed her parents for ruining her religious vocation, and retired to her room, which became her cloister. As time passed, nothing remained but the outer shell of good manners; underneath she nursed a vendetta against life. Dorothy lived and died in the house in Union City.

As gothic aunt Dorothy's life grew more uneventful, she spent her time dawdling in the past, reliving—and subtly revising—her early life. Its few highlights passed continually in review before her cold resentful eye. She'd bemoan the time she felt inner promptings from the Lord but was told she had buck teeth and that Jesus wouldn't find her pleasing.

She made life miserable for Deirdre—they all lived in the same big old house. Any originality in speech or clothing, any spontaneous playfulness was put down as immoral.

When Dorothy died, Deirdre and her mother got the house; they also got aunt Dorothy's ghost. According to Stan, crockery, knives and forks were lifted by an unseen force and hurled at Deirdre.

"One night," Deirdre's mother said, "I went into my daughter's bedroom while she was sleeping. There I see Dorothy's fetch, hovering over Dee's sleeping body."

"Well," I said, "what did you do?"

"I chased the intruder away," she replied without hesitation.

But now the most telling detail of this story. According to Deirdre, aunt Dorothy, in her last years, *wore nothing but black.* (Her costume in my nightmare.) Moreover, she was forever accusing her niece of being *in league with Satan!* (The words the apparition spoke to me!)

14

This experience jolted me out of my complacent idea of evil; it seemed to me I'd caught a glimpse into the lower depths of Dante's inferno. It was enough to make me wish there was no life after death. Extinction seemed preferable to bumping into Aunt Dorothy again.

The same ignorance makes me so bold as to deny absolutely the truth of the various ghost stories, and yet with the common, though strange, reservation that while I doubt any one of them, still I have faith in the whole of them taken together.

Immanuel Kant
Dreams of a Ghost-Seer

Chapter Sixteen
Memories of the Dead

My uncle was dying. He was my godfather, a barber by profession, and my father's old friend. Uncle Tony was warm-souled, given to gentle laughter, a man who enjoyed a glass of wine after a long day's work. Wasted with bone cancer, he lay in a hospital bed on New York's East Side. I paid him a visit, swapping a few words. A faint smile played on his lips. He looked like a man on painkillers, hovering between this world and the next. I stayed a while, then said goodbye.

He died a few weeks later. I hadn't seen him for ten years. I had strayed from aunts and uncles, cousins and other relatives. But I felt like visiting my uncle; I remembered he took care of me when I was a boy.

2

I missed my uncle's funeral, and he receded from my thoughts. A few months later I had a vivid dream of him. What stuck in my mind was his shirt—a red velvet hunting shirt. As if to call attention to itself, it glowed and sparkled. In the dream, my attention was riveted to this sparkling shirt. The image stayed with me for days, till I decided to call my uncle's wife.

I described the shirt, as I saw it in the dream, to my aunt. "I guess you wouldn't know about Uncle Tony's shirt." My uncle had a favorite red velvet hunting shirt—a gift from his son. I knew nothing about this. So why the dream?

My thought, reflecting on the shirt that seemed to call attention to itself, was that my uncle remembered me—the godson who visited him on his deathbed—and decided to return the courtesy. A last goodbye, a last attempt to fix a memory—before dropping into the sea of oblivion.

Of course, that's not the only interpretation. It's possible I learned of the shirt via telepathy from my living aunt's mind, and staged the dream to convince myself that my uncle had survived death. Maybe I needed to believe that somehow there was still an unbroken bond.

Whatever the right interpretation, I am struck by the tenacity of this unconscious inventor, so clever at remembering, so ingenious at the byways of telepathy. Some part of my soul apparently wants me to have an image of continuity, a sense of connectedness with the dead. It is, I suspect, this image of continuity, this sense of a lasting bond that the soul wants more than mere "proof" of life after death.

3

Needless to say, the incident won't sway the skeptic. For me, the *feel* of the experience was uncanny, the ingenuity of the unconscious mind calling up memories of the dead.

Another incident I find harder to explain as a sly maneuver of the subliminal mind: Once more the setting was the house on Woodlawn Avenue. One hot summer night, it was so stifling I got out of bed, and stretched out on the living-room floor. Exposed to three windows, I waited for a breeze, and soon fell asleep.

Dawn broke through the window, waking me. I opened my eyes with the impression that someone was in the room with me. I looked up. My dead grandmother was staring at me. Beside her was the phantom of another woman.

They were both looking at me. They seemed, in fact, to be looking right through me. They looked intently, yet without emotion.

My grandmother, the shorter woman, looked younger than she was when she died: her skin clear, her eyes blue, her blond hair now silver-tinted. Grandma was an outrageously vain woman, prone to fits of jealousy in her eighties.

But who was the woman beside her? Taller, her hair looked thicker. She wore a lace ribbon round her neck and a long blue dress. Her face, less round than my grandmother's, was finely cut.

The woman resembled my mother—a fact I noted half-consciously. Curious and self-absorbed, she stood there, as though she were in deep thought. The two phantoms lingered in the dawn light for a few seconds, then vanished.

4

"That sounds like your great aunt Kate. They always said she looked like me," remarked my mother when I described the apparition.

A photo I had never seen, taken early in the century, showed three women and two men; I immediately recognized one of the faces as the face of the woman I saw that morning. The photo showed my great grandmother and grandfather, a boy in knickers between them—and two girls. One of the girls was my grandmother when she was about thirteen. Standing beside her, the taller, thinner figure of her sister, Kate, about eighteen. No question in my mind—the face in the photo was the face of the apparition, although in the apparition, the woman I saw was in her forties. I was sure it was the same face.

I had never seen my great aunt, yet I was able to recognize her from an old photograph—from a photograph taken when she was a teenager.

5

I learned one interesting detail. My great aunt Kate once did *almost see me.* Aunt Kate visited our home when I was an infant, over thirty years before the time of the apparition. When she tried to take a peek at me, she was asked to back off. My mother was embarrassed by the old crib I was sleeping in, and pretended I was a light sleeper. My aunt Kate probably thought I was too poor a specimen to exhibit in the light of day.

She never saw me again. Maybe she and my grandmother, in some free moment of their afterdeath meanderings, decided to visit me that hot summer morning in Jersey City. Maybe Kate wanted to see for herself what sort of a fellow I turned out to be?

6

In any case, there is the puzzling fact that I matched the image in the photograph with the apparition. One way to explain this—assuming I never saw Kate or her photo—is to say that I obtained it by telepathy from the unconscious mind of some living person. With that information I could then conjure up an apparition of the two ladies.

On this interpretation, I may have indeed seen a phantom replica of a women I never met in my life; however, I would have seen it through the mind of a living person. In that case, we needn't suppose that aunt Kate survived death.

I've said little of telepathy, the least spectacular of paranormal phenomena. And yet telepathy is a strong basis for restoring the idea of the soul to its ancient dignity and splendor. Telepathy, as some philosophers have argued, puts the great bugbear of materialism at bay—if not out of court.

Contrary to popular ideas, there is no reason to believe that telepathy—direct mind to mind "contact"—is propagated by any form of radiant energy. For one thing, neither distance nor physical barriers block the telepathic "signal." Besides, thoughts, meanings, feelings, just aren't the *kinds* of things that could be coded in *any* physical mechanism.

7

The idea of telepathic "leakage" of thought from a living mind implies what Heraclitus said in his oracular way, five hundred years before the birth of Christ: We don't know the boundaries of our souls. Once you admit psychic leakage from one mind to another, the idea of bounded egos falls to pieces. We don't know the boundaries because we don't know the limits of influence between souls.

The telepathic interpretation of my experience suggests strange capacities of the human soul. For instance, it suggests that a kind of psychic replica of my great aunt existed in the mind of one or more living persons.

This "great aunt" replica mimics the appearance, the voice and speech mannerisms, even the aesthetic and emotional tone of the actual woman.

The phantom of a woman, now dead, thus lives on in the unconscious memory of the living. Moreover, this living soul replica of a human being apparently can jump from one mind to another—without the benefit of any physical mechanism.

What we call telepathy is remarkable stuff! Current scientific theory has yet to explain it. It suggests, as in the example of aunt Kate, that there exist living forms of mental life *already* unshackled from space and time, forms that move freely in a metaphysical twilight zone.

There may be all sorts of creatures afoot in this region of being, once we grant that the soul has unknown, possibly unlimited powers. The zoology of the future will have to study them.

My conclusion to these chapters on death: If such creatures of soul inhabit the gaps between physical brains—if telepathy is a fact of nature—can life after death be far behind?

To know the universe itself as a road, as
many roads, as roads for travelling souls.
Walt Whitman
Song of the Open Road

CONCLUSION
The Soul
in Evolution

"**Y**ou would not find out the boundaries of soul, even by travelling along every path: so deep a measure does it have." Heraclitus was right. The truth about the boundaries of soul remains unknown.

In this book, I have recounted experiences that widen our perception of those boundaries: In the official worldview, people aren't supposed to fly out of their bodies or know the future or encounter mysterious lights in the sky or see apparitions of the dead. Such things are officially forbidden. Since these experiences, and others I've reported, changed my idea of the soul's boundaries, I use the word "soulmaking" to describe them. Experiences are "soulmaking" if they shatter our routine image of self or soul, if they undo our fixed ideas of who and what we are—if they move and stir up the soul's depths.

The fact is that thousands, if not millions, of people are having soulmaking experiences. The boundless sea of the Heraclitean soul is awash with all sorts of queer and puzzling fish.

2

Soulmaking, as I see it, is the only war worth fighting for—the war to reclaim the soul's riches and depths. A metaphysical war, hostilities escalated with the rise of modern science; since the 17th century, science has gradually written soul off the map of "reality." At the academic front, it's been discarded, called with contempt the "ghost in the machine."

Nevertheless, the unconscious has a genius for forcing us to experience soul and her depths in unforeseen ways. Soul-enhancing and soul-discovering experiences are undoubtedly on the rise. Are we breaking through to a new consciousness of soul?

3

If there is a breakthrough, it is because of a breakdown—a reaction to collective soul loss. In our culture, loss of soul is evident in many ways. How often do we hear people say things like: "I took the job, but my soul wasn't in it," or "We were married for years, but our relationship lacked soul," or "That old street I once loved has lost its soul."

A new poetics of soul loss cries out for articulation—a new cartography of the soulless. Wherever we travel in the world today, we see signs and symptoms of it, a creeping soullessness in our everyday lives, an erosion of enchantment. Living without soul may well be the most dangerous undiagnosed disease of our time.

Soulmaking, in its natural simplicity, is merely the celebration of aliveness; yet at the same time, it is a form of social criticism. Making soul means speaking out against the spiritual totalitarians who want to jail the anomalies—the "outlaws"—in the life of our experience. However, the real concern isn't with any particular "anomalous" event. Something bigger is at stake—the right to be exceptional—the right to go one's way among the many roads of unbounded Heraclitean soul life.

4

Soulmaking is a fluid process; it is about redefining our images of reality. As such it is metaphysics in action, an exercise in reshaping our vision of who we are—of what we are becoming. The soul that Socrates and Jesus valued has a life of its own. We have to respect the law of that life. It's a day-to-day struggle, "making" our souls—defining but also undefining, realizing but also unrealizing ourselves. A process riddled with risk and ambiguity.

5

The idea of soulmaking has a history. Keats gave us the word and spoke of life itself as a "vale of soulmaking." It came to him in the spring of 1819 during a time of poetic ferment. About to write his greatest odes, Keats contrasted his idea of soulmaking to the way he knew as Christianity, which postponed experience of divinity to the next world. For Keats we are already "sparks of divinity" and need to rub ourselves against the pains and irregularities of jagged existence, before the sparks can burst into flames.

The idea of soulmaking is deep in our culture. We find it in Plato's Allegory of the Cave, in Book Seven of the *Republic,* which contains an account of the soul's fight to escape bondage to false consciousness. It is not easy and the terrifying truth is that the average "cave" dweller is more inclined to kill than hail his liberator—so disorienting is the experience of illumination.

Among the early Christian fathers, Iranaeus had an evolutionary conception of soulmaking. "We were not made gods at our beginning," he said, "but first we were made men, then, in the end, gods." Global theologian John Hick has today taken up the Iranaean view of soulmaking in a valiant effort to make sense of evil in a universe supposedly made by an all-loving Christian God. We need a hard, challenging world to test our souls, to awaken our power of choice and draw out our god-likeness, Hick contends.

When Saint Augustine was in Rome in 388 he wrote a treatise on soulmaking called *De Quantitate Animae.* Augustine maps the progress of soul: the first step in to experience sheer animation; then we awaken to sensory and rational life; then learn to bring order to our loves; then, if we keep on progressing, we acquire an appetite for the kind of knowledge that truly liberates; finally, drawn to the highest good, we end by ecstatically uniting our souls with God.

6

One point the traditional soulmaker insisted upon: this life, this one brief earthly life, is for most of us not enough to complete the opus of the soul's evolution. An afterlife is necessary. On this point, I have, at least to my own satisfaction, re-opened the door. In fact, it's all I claim: that the door is open. It may only be slightly ajar—but that is enough for me.

7

Many people I meet feel the spur of what we might call the evolutionary imperative. We are at a strange juncture today in the history of life on earth. It appears we're in the early stages of an unprecedented breakdown—of traditional societies and of the natural ecologies that support life. Many of us know of these impending perils, but relatively few of us are doing anything about it.

On the other hand, there are many exceptions. Many people believe they have a mission. They sense encroaching catastrophe. They may have had unusual experiences, not unlike those depicted in this book, experiences that leave them with a sense of unfinished business. Often, they retreat from their jobs, even from their friends and family; they seem to want to disengage from old habits, old values, old lifeways. Sometimes they grope blindly, scratching in the desert for water. And they may feel guilty, confused, disoriented.

Yet a strange energy often takes hold of them, prompting them to make big changes in their lives, driving them toward something they sense is critically important—something new and unknown and absolutely necessary. They are on the move—their souls are moved. The direction may not be clear; only the feeling of urgency to go on—to advance.

Such people may be feeling the spur of an evolutionary imperative. An obscure voice within is prodding many of us to break ranks and reach for new forms of soul life. What sort of forms? I think the answer is clear: Forms that will help us to survive in the awesome world we have created.

Most people who have thought about our predicament agree that we need a revolution—or if you like—an evolution of consciousness. Earth itself has a vested interest in such a venture. A new consciousness is needed to tip the balance toward saving planet Earth; taking our inner evolution in hand may be our best hope. Soulmaking, seen in this light, is an evolutionary imperative.

8

For me, soulmaking begins with questioning the Shadow. We need to face the dark side of ourselves, the side yet shrouded in denial: the scary stuff hidden in old closets; the unbidden and forbidden dreams; the alien impulses, weird fantasies that ring the candle flame of ordinary consciousness, threatening to snuff it out.

The soul must face its ignorance, its powerlessness before unconscious forces, its nighttime and noontide potentials. And so I have focused here on the intruders—the barbarians from the far side of the psyche.

Science calls them "anomalies." Anomalies are reminders that we're flanked on all sides by metaphysical outlaws—creatures that elude our grasp and control. Who knows what forms of being brush shoulders with us? What Angels of the Shadow sleep at our side? Our strange encounters offer us an opportunity to dialogue with these intruders.

9

I have been asked about rules of thumb for soulmakers: the first rule is fidelity to personal experience. If we want to explore the forgotten depth of the Heraclitean soul, we have to be faithful to our experiences. Official science is only faithful to the repeatable—

the controllable elements of experience. But the unrepeatable, the uncontrollable, have the power to push us beyond the edges of ourselves.

I choose fidelity to my quirky encounters with reality. As a result, the world I've come to entertain as "real" looks a little more like Alice's Wonderland than I would have guessed after reading Alfred Korzybski's "Science and Sanity."

10

One of the great lessons of soulmaking deals with the dance of opposites. Carl Jung, the father of modern soulmaking, thought becoming a "whole" human being meant working through opposites; he saw the "self" as a fourfold structure made up of two pairs of opposing forces: thought and feeling, intuition and sensation. This may sound a little too pat, but may alert us to our penchant for onesidedness.

Onesidedness in the enemy of soulmaking. We become caricatures of parts of ourselves: We are too thoughtful or too passionate, too given to airy intuition or too chained to hard sense. What Jung called *individuation* is the ideal of bringing the four forces of the soul into a state of dynamic interplay.

Dance—not balance: The "balance" metaphor seems too mechanical. We don't really want to be perfectly balanced; for if all our forces are in equilibrium, we are near death. I don't want to *add* feeling or *subtract* thinking; I want my feelings molded by thought and my thoughts animated by feeling. Nor do I want to *divide* sensory experience or *multiply* intuition; I want to test my intuitions with the wealth of sensory experience, and see through sensory experience with the light of intuition. Opposites in interplay, strengthening each other's virtues, chastening each other's vices.

11

In my judgment, the modern soulmaker has a special affinity to the feminine. You may have noticed that many of the stories in this book had some tie-in with women. I used to dream of a mysterious woman who rescued me from hideous monsters. I grew up listening to psychic stories from my mother. My grandma and great aunt haunted me. A woman friend's ghost attacked me. A woman in her astral double rearranged my furniture. It was love of woman that inspired my flight of trans-atlantic astral sex. A woman shared with me the story of her magical child. The century's most amazing aerial phenomena involve the figure of a goddess. I was with a woman when my tropical plant flowered anomalously, and with a woman when I witnessed a UFO in Greenwich Village. And thanks to a woman I saw through the psychodrama of the Jesus-Satan archetype.

What's the link between the psychic and the feminine? One link is pretty obvious. If you research psychic phenomena, you're going to run into lots of women. Women are more willing to admit they have psychic experiences and less afraid of them than men seem to be.

But the link is deeper. The feminine, in a man, reflects his unconscious life—his anima or soul. Fear of the feminine is thus fear of the soul—of the "psychic." The soulmaker has to overcome this fear, which is a fear of surrender, a fear of losing control.

12

The "higher" religions like to warn us of the dangers of the psychic. But what of the dangers of the spiritual? Lucifer was no crystal-ball huckster! He was supreme in the realm of spiritual perfection. The truth is that psyche and spirit are as closely intertwined as magic and religion.

Psychic faculty increases receptivity to signals of spiritual transformation. One purpose the kind of event discussed in this book may be to wear down one's resistance to the world of spirit. Psi events show us the incompleteness of our normal sense of reality.

Paranormal phenomena erode the self-sufficiency and supposed rationality of the infamous "male ego." The increase of all kinds of psychic phenomena in the world today, for all we know, may have this very purpose: To heat up the dance of opposites between the masculine and the feminine, between the Shiva of searching intellect and the Shakti of embracing soul.

13

Dreams are crucial to the soulmaker's art. Our greatest onesidedness is to cling to consciousness, to the ideas we use to tame the wilderness we call experience.

Love of ideas reached a peak for me while I was studying philosophy at Columbia University. By day I honed the skills of academic philosophy; by night I was haunted by dreams that painted pictures of alternate realities.

Dream the dream onwards! Jung said. Let the images of the dream go where they want to. Let them unravel themselves spontaneously, without interference from our conscious minds. Jung called this "active imagination." Active imagination is the dialogue we conduct with the intelligence that cloaks itself behind the messengers of the unconscious. Dreams are one powerful form this dialogue often takes.

14

Crucial to the fine art of soulmaking is how we relate to our native spiritual traditions. We can't make ourselves over into new and whole human beings without wrestling with the angels of our native spiritual traditions.

I find symbols, images, and energies of my Catholic tradition appearing within myself from time to time—and I find they exert pushes and pulls on my soul life. To ignore them would be to ignore a part of myself. But the rule for soulmakers is not to be absorbed by one idea, one force. Like everything in the living synthesis of soulmaking, the spiritual beliefs we inherit by chance must be critically integrated—but with love and respect.

In our age of mounting ethnic warfare, we need to learn to steer through many nations in the commonwealth of soul. As we let the opposites within us dance freely together, so we must travel through all the "chakras," at one with our lower and our higher energies, embracing yet transcending all the influences— all the signs and houses of the inner zodiac. In this way we might learn to move toward a true catholicism of the soul.

15

So telling tales about psychic anomalies is no idle pastime. The purpose in this book is to recover the forgotten dimensions of our souls.

We live in challenging times, and a new consciousness is struggling to emerge. This new consciousness sees itself in the vanguard of evolution. We must evolve, say the new visionaries, or perish.

Life, they say, demands a new vision of itself—of its future. For life has entered a new kind of danger zone. To pass beyond it we have to pass beyond egoism to soulfulness, beyond tribal to cosmic consciousness. For this we need to build a new society of soulmakers. The deeper we all descend into our souls, the easier it will be for us to rise together. As Heraclitus said long ago: "The way up and the way down are one and the same."

Dr. Grosso welcomes correspondence
on soulmaking experiences. Write:

**Michael Grosso, Ph.D.
26 Little Brooklyn Road
Warwick, NY 10990**